Luther Corhern's
Salmon Camp Chronicles

UNIVERSITY OF WINNIPEG, 515 Portage Ave., Winnipeg, MB. R3B 2E9 Canada

Luther Corhern's Salmon Camp Chronicles

Herb Curtis

GOOSE LANE

Published by Goose Lane Editions with the assistance of the Canada Council, the Department of Canadian Heritage, and the New Brunswick Department of Economic Development, Tourism and Culture, 1999.

Edited by Laurel Boone.
Cover illustration by Judi Pennanen.
Cover photograph © Thomas R. Pero, 1999. Reproduced with permission of the photographer.
Cover design by Julie Scriver.
Book design by Ryan Astle.
Printed in Canada by Transcontinental Printing.
10 9 8 7 6 5 4 3 2

Canadian Cataloguing in Publication Data

Curtis, Herb, 1949-
   Luther Corhern's salmon camp chronicles

ISBN 0-86492-268-X
I. Title.

PS8555.U842L88 1999   C813.'54   C99-950045-7
PR9199.3.C826L88 1999

Goose Lane Editions
469 King Street
Fredericton, New Brunswick
CANADA   E3B 1E5

To Shari

Contents

Luther Corhern's
Salmon Camp Chronicles

Call Me Luther

I never met a fisherman in my life (other than Stan Tuney) who would tell you a lie. And I, Luther Corhern, one of the very best salmon fishermen to ever wet a line in the Miramichi River, am not about to change things.

Before we get going, I suppose I should introduce myself, fill you in on what kind of an all-round good lad I am. I was born and raised on the Hemlock Road, in the little settlement of Big Spring, on the banks of the Miramichi River. Big Spring has a population of fifty-six people, seventeen dogs, eleven cats, and a bunch of farm animals like horses, pigs, cows, and chickens that I never really got around to counting. We also have about a million salmon that visit us every year, and quite a few Americans.

Our settlement has one small general store and the one-room school I attended for ten long years. I finally graduated, and that made me one of the more educated lads in the settlement. After school I travelled a bit, mostly to various towns and cities in the Maritimes, but eventually came home and went into the paddle-making business. I also became a bait salesman and started selling worms to all the fishermen that came to our famous river to fish. Bait selling was a pretty good business, too, for a few years, but like so many successful small businessmen, I got screwed by the government. Some politician got it into his head that the Miramichi River and all its tributaries should be fly-fishing-only rivers, and, sure enough, that's what happened. Now, it takes no stretch of the imagination to figure out how this legislation choked the worm business. I was ruined! Oh, I tried selling squirrel tails and feathers for tying flies for a while, but squirrels, ducks, robins, chickadees and the like are a lot harder to come by than worms. Eventually I was forced to close up my shop completely.

That's when I decided to become a guide.

Being a guide means I don't have to do much of anything other than stay within yelling distance of some American sport. For instance, while my sport is out there beating the water, I usually just sit around on the shore in the shade, fight a few flies, snooze now and again, and yell out stuff like, "Take off that Cosseboom and tie on a Green Machine!" or "You're out too far! Move down six feet!"

Once in a while, if there's a run on, and if the sport can throw a line worth looking at, I might have to scoop the occasional fish, coaching the sport all the time — "Hold 'im high! Don't force 'im! Keep yer rod up!" and whatever else he or she might need to know. Guiding, you see, is the very best of a job. Anyway, that's about all the work anyone could get out of me until just lately. Lately, much to my surprise, I became a logger.

Now, you might be wondering what logging has to do with guiding salmon fishermen. Well, you see, logging isn't really what I'm doing. I mean, I'm not about to go out in the woods and work like the devil cutting logs. No, boys, that kind of work is not for a lad like me who can read and write. No, that kind of work is for the others, the lads I hang around with, Nean, Lindon, Shad, Lyin' Stan Tuney, Elvis, lads like that. And now I suppose you're wondering what in the name of God I'm coming at, first saying I'm a logger and then saying I'm not.

Well, it's a little bit of a story. It starts way back with my daddy, who was born and raised right here on the Miramichi River, just like myself. But, unlike me, he was no slouch of a man when it came to working — logging, planting potatoes, farming, running a power saw, carpentry — you know, real work.

Miramichi, by the way, is thought to be an Indian word meaning "happy meeting place where it's cold as a moose yard in the winter and blueberries and crabapples are plentiful in the summer; the place where salmon swim and court and make love in the fall." However, I happen to know that Miramichi is not an Indian word at all. It is taken from the Latin word *mirus*, which means that it's a nice place to fish, it's easy to get to, and the rates aren't too bad.

My mother first introduced me to the Miramichi. She made the river out to be a mysterious and dangerous place, harbouring savage Indians and child-stealing Gypsies. She led me to believe that it was black and cold and deep and vicious, a thing that would swallow you up if you were to go anywhere near it.

Every year the river claimed someone, it seemed — a guide upset his canoe, a sport waded too deep, a child was caught too far out, another was pulled by an undertow, a lumberjack fell from a log while on the drive. All grist for my mother's stay-away-from-the-river mill. I can still hear her warnings:

"Don't go near that river and get drownt!"

"Stay away from that river, ya hear!"

"The Indians will get ya!"

"There's Gypsies down there!"

"Don't you know it's dog days? The first thing ya know you'll fall in that river and get polio!"

While other children dealt with the boogeyman, ghosts in the closet, and things that go bump in the night, I had to deal with the Miramichi River. I was ten, I think, before I realized that the local Native people did not steal children and that Gypsies may have passed through the Miramichi area once or twice and maybe not.

It was the stories of danger that kindled my imagination.

Maybe I was naturally contrary, but the more my mother insisted that the river was a nasty, scary place, the more it lured me, the more attractive it seemed. That's why I learned to pole a boat when I was eight, could swim like a fish by the time I was ten, and at twelve could cast ninety feet of Cortland 444.

My father never did much to introduce me to the river. He wanted me to work for a living. What he called work was chopping and plowing and sawing and sweating. What my father called work did not include sitting in the shade on the bank of the Miramichi River guiding rich Americans.

Picture it. You're a child of perhaps eight. You live in an isolated little community, and the Miramichi River — a river so clean that you can drink its water, that is so full of fish its surface is constantly dappled with movement — flows by not more than two hundred yards from your door. From one set of lips you hear stories of danger and mystery. And from other sets of lips you're hearing things like, "Stan Tuney caught a twenty-pounder last night!"

I tell you, if the devil had lived in that river, I would have been his sidekick from way back. And you know something? I wouldn't blame the devil if he did hang out on the Miramichi, for, with its great forests and lush meadows, sometimes lit by fireflies and moonlight, it's always a pretty thing to look at and a nice, gentle place to be.

Now, the logger thing. Well, I was guiding an American by the name of Cavender Bill from way down in the States (we call him Cav), and we were sitting around the Salmon Camp (which is what he calls his cottage) chewing the rag, smoking, having a warm Moosehead, and Cav says, "Wow! Those yarns ya'll are telling are something else. With all the fish stories going around, we should be keeping a log." And Bert (The Loon) Coleford speaks right up and agrees with him. "Yes, sir, that's fer sure, yeah, we should. Keep a log, yeah. Know any-one kin write?"

Lindon Tucker says, "Write? Write? Lute here's the boy what kin write!" Lindon and the boys are apt to call me anything other than Luther — Lute, Loon Fart, Chub Face, Egg Head — but it doesn't matter a sign in the world what they call me, as long as I know that the salmon are running and what fly they're catching them on.

Lindon knew I could write, you see, because I used to write his letters to his aunt in Fredericton: "How are you? I am fine. Hope you are the same," every letter worded pretty much the same. So that's why he pointed the finger at me.

"Well, I'm not much at writing and stuff like that," I said.

"Well, ya'll don't have to do that much, Luther, my boy," said Cav. "Just jot down a few things about the guests who stay here at the Salmon Camp, how many fish are being caught. You know, just write down what's going on."

"Well, I don't know."

"What don't you know, boy? You can do it."

"Oh, I couldn't."

"Sure you can. Hell's bells, I'd do it mahseff, if I wasn't busier than a cow's ass in flah time." Cavender Bill, being an American, had a funny way of talking.

"But today, nothing happened."

"That don't mattah a fiddler's wink, boy! When the boys read about themselves, they'll be as tickled as a loon in an eel's nest! And I reckon mah guests would get a kick out of it, too. What d'ya say, boy?"

"Well, I don't know . . ."

"Say, Luther, ya'll ever get around to havin' a belt of that bourbon I brought all the way from Texas? I think I still have darn near a case of it somewhere . . ."

* Log *

June 24

8:00 A.M. One salmon. 21 pounds. Caught by Lindon Tucker's sport, a lad by the name of Lefty Devito from Chicago. Caught in the Home Pool behind the Furlong Rock.

8:45 A.M. One grilse. Five pounds. Caught by Lefty Devito in the Home Pool behind the Bellyview Rock. Lefty caught limit, left river, then the other sports went to the pool. It seems Lefty likes fishing alone. That's all right with all the guides other than Lindon Tucker. As long as Lefty doesn't catch any fish, the rest of us can sleep in.

11:15 A.M. One salmon. Nine pounds. Caught by Bert Coleford's sport, Giselle Poirier from Montreal. A pretty little thing, the salmon, I mean. Caught behind Aunt Sally's Rock.

2:15 P.M. One salmon. 42 pounds. Caught by Cavender Bill. Caught in the Home Pool behind the Furlong Rock. There was only Cav and me there when he landed it. We released it, of course.

Cav gave me a raise in pay for keeping this log for him.

I know Daddy would want me to make something better of myself than a writer of what's going on in the Salmon Camp, so I told him I was a logger. I didn't lie a whole lot, no more than a fellow would down on the bank of the river. I'm not about to start lying, me being a salmon fisherman and all.

Luther Corhern

We Call Him Cavender Bill

The other day I was sitting here on the veranda of the Salmon Camp, fighting flies and one-fingering my log on my old Remington, when I heard something squeak behind me, smelled something kind of fishy, and felt a hand touch my shoulder. It was cold, felt more like a salmon's tail brushing across me than an actual human hand.

I froze right then and there for a good solid minute, and I was nearly blue in the face from holding my breath and listening for whatever ghost it might belong to before Lotty speaks up and says, "How's the log comin', Lute?"

Hearing and knowing it was Lotty felt some good, I tell ya, for Lotty's a lot of things, but she's not a ghost — not yet, anyway.

Lotty's the camp cook, and she'd been cleaning a couple of shad for lunch, which was why her hands were cold, like a ghost's. I should have known it was Lotty, for she's been touching me a lot lately, ever since I showed her my nine-footer that I bought brand spanking new from Elvis. She likes a man who knows what he wants, you see, and I wanted that fishing rod and . . . well . . . she knew it.

"Yes, Lotty, dear, I'm trying to get the log together, and I'd appreciate it if ya didn't sneak up and touch a man. With your hands all cold like that and smellin' of fish, I thought you were old John Cavender!"

"Old John Cavender's been dead for fifty years!" said Lotty.

"That's what I mean. I thought you was him."

"Sorry, Lute."

"Oh, it's all right, Lotty, dear. Don't worry about it."

I like Lotty the very best, and of course she wants to keep touching a high-toned lad like me. I mean, how many other lads around here operate a Remington, write logs, and have a new nine-foot Shakespearean graphite fishing rod to show for it?

Anyway, I thought at first she was a ghost.

It's not that I'm all that superstitious, you understand. It's where I was sitting that helped conjure my case of the willies. If it had been three years ago instead of three days, there probably would have been a ghost there, sure enough, and I wouldn't have taken all the nine-footers you could lug in a transport truck to write my log in that particular location.

Wrap your tongue around this: Wilhelm Washington Nagyrapolt. That's the American lad's name who bought the old Cavender homestead four years ago, built the Salmon Camp, and started keeping sports. He's the lad who hired all us lads to guide and gave me a raise in pay for keeping the camp log. Wilhelm Washington Nagyrapolt. Quite a mouthful. I just used up about a yard of ribbon typing it. And there's not one lad around here who can pronounce it, including myself. All us lads call him Cavender Bill.

When Cav bought this place, the first thing he did was tear down the old house. I figure she had about forty-two ghosts in her, and, having no place to stay all of a sudden, every one of them moved up across the field and settled into the old Clowater house. Stan Tuney said he saw them crossing the field, all wearing white sheets and looking very scary.

Cavender Bill's a pretty good lad, has a nice place here, two pools with lots of salmon in them and a pretty good run of sports. All spring, summer, and fall, he keeps us lads busier than a hen hauling wood. And even when he's having a bad day, like the time Stan Tuney stepped on his rod and blamed it on Nean, he's better to have around than a bunch of ghosts.

He doesn't mind us calling him Cavender Bill. I think he

even likes it. I mean, a lad would have to like being called just about anything at all, if he had a name like that mouthful of crabapples.

And he has names for us, too. Little pet names. It's his way of getting more work out of us, I think. When he calls me Lute, for instance, I'll do more for him than I would if he called me Luther. You know, it's like he's one of the boys.

Last year, Hogarth Glasby got himself a job guiding here, and one day we were eating in the kitchen — potatoes, fiddle-heads, and salmon with chow chow and a wedge of lemon on the side. Lotty always puts lemon on your plate when she serves fish, and mostly nobody ever eats it. But this day, Hogarth decided he'd try it and sucked it right back just as if it was an orange. Well, as you may imagine, his face went every which way, his nose all wrinkled up, and for about five minutes afterwards he sat there with kind of a sneer on his face. A lemon will do that to you.

In came Cavender Bill.

"What's the matter with you, Hogarth?" he said. "You look like Elvis Presley."

Although he still had the sneer, Hogarth had more or less forgotten the lemon and thought Cav was telling him that he was good looking, complimenting him by comparing him with someone no less handsome than the King of Rock and Roll himself.

So Hogarth wore the sneer for the rest of the day. The next day he came to work with his hair all greased back and his collar turned up. It wasn't more than a week or two before we all noticed that he had lowered his sideburns a couple of inches.

We all caught on to what was happening right away, of course. We started calling him Elvis on a regular basis, and Hogarth bit into the concept even more. Last fall he painted his pickup truck pink, and even though his wife's name is

Marguerite, he wrote "Miss Prisella" across the hood just above the grill. Two weeks ago he sold me his nice new Shakespearean graphite and bought himself a leather jacket with the money.

And then there's Belvin Kooglin.

Belvin's a great big lad, six and a half feet tall, weighs over two hundred and fifty pounds, and is kind of round-shouldered like me. He's a guide, a part-time lumberjack, and a would-be carpenter, but if you were to ask him what he did for a living, he'd tell you he's an inventor, claims to have invented some kind of a fly for waders, a zipper that won't leak. He won't show you the waders, of course, because he's afraid you might steal his brilliant idea. So it's all a big mystery for us lads, and none of us, even Cavender Bill, who's been just about everywhere, can figure out how it could possibly work. I mean, if water can't get in, how are you gonna get your pecker out?

Anyway, one day Belvin, Stan, Dryfly, Lindon, Elvis, and I were all sitting around in the shade talking to Cav, waiting for the Strindberg party to come in from Massachusetts, and Cav says, "You know, boys, angling is as old as man. They claim Neanderthal was the first angler."

"Nean who?" asked Belvin.

"Neanderthal. Caught his daily quota by means of a gorge, a straight piece of bone with a line attached to it. The fish would swallow the gorge, and before he got around to regurgitating it, old Neanderthal yanked him right out of the water and up on the bank. We can thank Neanderthal for a great many inventions."

And then he looks at Belvin, kind of grins, and says, "You know, Belvin my boy, I think Neanderthal might very well have been a relative of yours."

Belvin liked that, I tell ya. Grinned from ear to ear. Thinks inventing runs in his family.

Good old Nean.

Well, it's getting late, I've heard the day's reports, so I guess

I'd better write the log. I'd like to tell you about Stan Tuney's boasting that he guided Santa Claus last spring, but, well, some other time.

* Log *

July 8

8:15 A.M. One grilse. 4 pounds. Caught by Alfonse McCormick. Caught in the Home Pool behind Aunt Sally's Rock on a No. 6 Green Machine. It's Alfonse's first day here and his first Atlantic salmon, and he's real proud. Got his picture taken twice.

9:45 A.M. One salmon. 8 pounds. Caught by Lindon Tucker's sport, Simon Lunt, from Atlanta, Georgia. Caught in the Home Pool behind the Furlong Rock on a No. 8 Smurf.

11: 25 A.M. One Grilt. 5 pounds. Caught by Blain O'Hara from New York City. Caught in the Home Pool behind the Bellyview Rock on a No. 6 Butterfly. The fish had a tag on it worth ten bucks. Some guys have all the luck.

8:00 P.M. One salmon. 9 pounds. Caught by Nean Glasby's sport, Noreen Palmer from Boston, Massachusetts. Caught in the Ramp Pool behind Head Rock on a No. 6 Blue Charm.

9:15 P.M. After everybody else left the Home Pool, Cavender Bill waded out and hooked his usual 37-pounder behind the Bellyview Rock. Said he hooked it on a big white, yellow, red and blue Bomber with an orange hackle.

Luther Corhern

The Convenient Store

Lying Stan Tuney opened up a small general store. It's the first one we've had since Dooper's General sort of slid into history along with old Billy.

On the first night it opened, Randy Stevens went over to buy some corned beef, and Stan stuck his chest right out like a bantam rooster and declared that he wouldn't be handling entrées.

"Entrées?" asked Randy.

"You see, the general store is a thing of the past," said Stan. "Nowadays, they're called convenient stores."

"Convenience stores," corrected Randy.

"Yeah. That's what I'm trying to say," said Stan. "And in a convenient store, ya don't sell corned beef."

"Why not?" asked Randy.

"Because corned beef is not considered to be a convenient item," explained Stan. "A convenient store is a place where ya get convenient things — ketchup, chow chow, wieners, canned stuff, potato chips, soda pop, TV dinners, Tums, stuff like that. Now, I could sell ya *canned* corn beef, if I had some . . . but I don't have it in stock yet."

"No, no, that's all right," said Randy. "I'll just drive into Doaktown and get the real stuff."

"Good. Now you're learnin'," said Stan. "You gotta try and stick with the times."

Stan's Convenient Store is where most of us lads spend our evenings these days. We're having a hell of a time trying to convince Stan that beer is considered convenient and that he should put up a dart board. "You're closer, so you're more convenient than the Legion" is our argument.

I don't really think Stan cares if he makes money or not. All he really wants to do is talk.

Stan's getting up there in years, gets the senior citizen's pension, and is pretty much retired from working in the woods and guiding. He's a nice old fellow, really. We call him Lying Stan Tuney because he never told the truth in his life, but we like him just the same. The older he gets, the more religious he gets and the more he tries to tell the truth, but it's just not in his nature. I don't know why he bothers to try — we all know when he's lying and have learned over the years that his lies are much more entertaining than whatever truths he might come up with if he searched really hard.

It must be a bit confusing for him, though, because he's told so many yarns so many times that he's forgotten which one was a lie to begin with. Not knowing whether you're lying or not must be a racket to deal with in the confession booth.

Anyway, he's opened up a little store with a sign over the door that reads "Stan's Convenient Store," and that's where we spend most of our evenings, eating potato chips, drinking pop, smoking, and trying to get a word in here and there when Stan's doing all the talking.

The other night, Lindon, Nean, Elvis, and I were all there, and Stan announced that he wasn't going to hunt anymore.

"Well," says Nean, "you are getting up there in years . . ."

"No, no, it ain't got nothin' to do with my age."

"You're becoming a vegetarian?" I asked.

"No, that's got nothin' to do with it, either. I just don't think man should kill animals. It's as plain and simple as that, and I've been giving it a lot of thought."

"Well, if you don't kill animals, then you must be considerin' being a vegetarian," argued Nean.

"I never said that," said Stan, getting a bit frustrated with our stupidity. "What I said is that I'm not gonna hunt anymore."

"Oh, we thought you were saying you're gonna quit killing . . ."

"I *am* saying that! Ya see, it's all right in my book to kill a cow or a rooster, they're just farm animals and are born and riz for killin'. But a deer or a partridge is a different matter. Man has no place in Mother Nature's territory."

"I think he's against trophy hunting," I suggested.

"That, too," said Stan.

"How, how, how, as the feller says, how about fishing?" asked Lindon.

"Now, now! I never said anything about fishin'! Fish are a different kind of an animal. But whales fit the no-hunting list. Whales are like moose or deer, did ya know that?"

"Mammals, you mean."

"You got it."

"So you kin sort of pick and choose," put in Elvis.

"Well, yeah. Now, I know what you're thinking. You think that I'm trying to convince you lads to pack your guns right up and quit huntin' just like I'm doin'. But you're wrong. I'm just sayin' that huntin' ain't for me. You know what turned me against it?"

"The porcupine?"

"Yeah, well . . . I put three bullets in the head of that porcupine in the middle of the night, and when I got up in the morning to go out and bury it so the dog wouldn't get into the quills, it was gone, vanished, disappeared. I looked all over . . . all over . . . all over . . ."

"Hell's creation?" I offered.

"That, my boy, is the worst kind of blasphemy! I looked all over the place for it. There wasn't as much as a speck of blood or a quill. Gone!"

"Then one evening you were fishin' up at the Hoge Pool with me, and when you went home, there it was," said Elvis.

"Layin' right, right, right on your doorstep, wasn't it, Stan?" added Lindon.

"Right on my doorstep! Flies buzzing around it, its head all shot up. Right there on my doorstep! Now, what do you think of that?"

"Maybe someone found it and put it there as a joke," suggested Elvis.

"No, sir! That thing came back there and died just to get even with me. It was what you call your omen."

"What if I told you that I put it there so you could bury it before your dog got into it?" asked Nean.

"I wouldn't believe ya. No man in his right mind is gonna pick up a dead porcupine. It was an omen, I tell ya! It was the good Lord's way of telling me that He's changed His mind about the killing of animals. It was His regulation to me."

"You mean revelation," I said.

"That's right! The good Lord's got a new set of rules and revelations. Entered my thoughts, He did, and told me that it's wrong to hunt. And I just forget, now, but I think He told me on that very same day that fishin's okay. If I got it right, I believe He told me that He did a bit of guidin' in the Bible, told His sports they were fishin' on the wrong side of the boat or something like that.

"Anyway, I believe that animals got intelligence just like us lads, and it ain't right to hunt them. Fish all you want, but huntin's out, a thing of the past just like the general store."

"What you said about whales a while ago, about them being mammals," I put in. "Have you heard about how one whale will try to save another whale that's in trouble?"

"Pretty likely!" said Stan. "That's what I'm sayin'! Didn't Jonah get saved by a whale?"

"Well, I don't know about Jonah," I said. "But not too long ago I had a sick goldfish, couldn't swim upright. So I checked the tank one evening, and there was one of the other fish swimming beside him, holding him up."

"So?"

"So I'm just telling you, you can't exclude fish from your list. Fish are as intelligent as mammals. A goldfish or a salmon is no different than a moose, a deer, or a partridge."

"Just what are you coming at, Lute? Are you sayin' the Lord is wrong?"

"No, I'm just saying that if you believe it's wrong to hunt, then you're a hypocrite if you don't quit fishing, too."

I was the one who brought this point of view to the surface, but Nean, Lindon, and Elvis also knew where I was coming from, and we all watched old Stan and waited for his reply.

We all knew that Stan would rather fish than eat, that if you took his fishing rod, you might as well shove it through his heart because he wouldn't live long without it anyway. Old Stan grew up and lived his entire life on the Miramichi River, and fly fishing is as much a part of his life as breathing. We're all like that. City folks go to the movies or the theatre, us lads go fishing.

But Stan was never one to let too much reality enter his head, and we didn't have to wait more than a second or two for his response.

"Well, that goldfish of yours was just checking out the sick one to see if it was dead," says Stan. "As soon as the sick one dies, that healthy one will eat him, sure as I'm standing here tryin' to reason with you lads. I can't believe you're that stupid! Fishin's our livelihood!"

"So is huntin', for some people," dared Nean.

"Ha! No, sir! A fish might try and save the life of another fish, but he ain't like a dog or a whale. A fish would let a man sink to the bottom and grin all the time he was watching. A fish ain't what you call your whachamacallit . . . a . . . a . . . "

"A mammal."

26

"Exactly. No, sir! From now on, I'm gonna fish, but I ain't gonna hunt. I'm gonna become what you might call a con-servationalist."

"Conversationalist, you mean," I kidded.

"Whatever."

Well, Elvis, Nean, Lindon, and I had some fun with the whole issue. Nean declared that he just might get rid of his old hound and get himself a whale instead, that he could maybe train the whale to sniff out a few salmon, just like his old dog sniffs out cats and the like.

Down deep inside, however, I thought it an interesting bit of ranting and raving. It never hurts to think about something like that once in a while.

The way I see it, old Stan is getting on and probably has reservations about going deep into the woods to hunt, and that's probably the real reason why he's giving it up. But, you know, as confusing as his whole perspective may be on the killing of mammals and such, I sort of know where he's coming from. When you catch a salmon, you can release it if you want. Put a bullet in a deer and it's all over.

I often think that a man should listen to what older people have to say, even if they're telling what you know are yarns.

Anyway, it's time I hit the hay. Cavender Bill and I are off to the Renous River bright and early in the morning.

* Log *

July 23

A hot sunny day like every other day for the last two weeks. No fish caught. Nobody even bothered to fish. However, word has it there are a few salmon being caught on the Renous.

Luther Corbern

The Secret

I'm going to unfold a secret. I'm coming out of the closet. To hell with it! Who cares? It's nothing to be ashamed of, and I'm tired of living a lie. Let it be revealed in the Salmon Log, since only about nine people read this, and most of you are friends, real friends, friends I can trust.

You know, life is sometimes sweet here. I've started reading books half the night. The first thing I do after awakening in the morning is take a bath, swim in the river in front of my trailer. I supplement my income as a guide with my little garden, the Swiss chard and carrots, the beets (sacred in my book), the zucchinis, cucumbers, corn, green beans and lettuce; the herbs, mushrooms and flowers . . .

Yes, I've done it! I'm guilty. But before you pass judgement, you found out first here in the Salmon Log.

It's summer, the time to hang loose. The river is low and calm. Every night you're haunted by scenes from the past, those youthful, hormone-influenced days when everything was beautiful. The moon rose, the sun set, friends laughed with you.

You might not believe me, but once I saw a man lie down on the floor beside his dog so he could cuddle it without disturbing its sleep. I know a woman who rises at four o'clock in the morning just so she can do her laundry and have it hanging on the line before everyone else. I know another guy who loves to fish but is afraid of the water, loves to hunt but is afraid of the forest. We all have our aversions, perversions, complexes, and idiosyncrasies, we all have our secrets. That's what makes us individuals.

It was the excitement and challenge that drew me into it. I recalled younger days when the mere mention of it would place a man on a social scale with the losers of wars: misrepresented, victimized by media, totally misunderstood.

Because of something, perhaps having to do with my molecular makeup, I love life and fear death. I love summer, when everything is warm, green, and alive. I hate winter, when everything is cold and dead. It's all natural, of course. I'm a human being with ears, feet, and a penis. I'm natural, too.

Only I'm not.

I blame it on the storms.

Forgive me for stooping to poetry, but storms are the essence of life, the twinkle in the eye, the arousal; storms are what enlivens the sea, makes men out of boys; storms demand respect. There's nothing more mediocre and disappointing than a storm without at least a bark. If it's gonna rain, let it pour.

Sometimes I think the most exciting things that happen to many of us are the storms we witness, encounter, fall victim to. Winter storms can be listened to and dealt with in many ways, but mostly they're just an inconvenience. I'm talking about summer storms here, thunder and lightning. I knew a guy who showered under the eaves of his house when it rained. He had a shower in his bathroom, but he did it anyway. Standing out there, naked, lathered up — I guess it was a back-to-the-earth thing, a freedom thing. I knew another guy who'd go into the swamp back of his house and watch the storms. I knew two idiots who would bike all day in the heavy rain.

Once I spent a whole day trying to write an appropriate poem to describe how rain made me feel. One verse went:

The dullest of moments would never exist,
If one really saw what there is in the mist.

Another attempt went:

Rain germinates and richly provides.
It washes the soil, the leaves, and the hides.

I wrote fifteen or twenty verses, none of which captured the feeling. I've tried it with music, too, and the closest I came was finding a chord on the guitar that sounded like rain falling into a tin barrel.

Rain.

How many times have people tried to explain the gentle, lulling music of the rain?

Rain.

Mournful music for the mind.

Whether you're standing naked under the eaves or biking down the road, wet as the back side of a little boy's ear, or supposing you're warm and cozy under a cabin roof, indoors or out, you feel the rain. Rain is a feeling. Thunder and lightning is a feeling. It's a good feeling, too. It stirs you.

It arouses me.

I think what happened to me came out of idleness. Maybe I was bored. Maybe I'm just making up excuses. The fact of the matter is, I'm guilty and I have to live with it. I thought at first it would be best kept a secret. Tuck it away as a moment of weakness and forget about it, I told myself. But what I did nags me, haunts me. The need to come out with it is driving me crazy.

I know you'll laugh when I tell you, and I'll blush every

time I see you on the street or in the grocery store, but the need to get it off my chest is just too great. I must tell you.

Hear my sigh. I'm gathering courage.

The other day was hot and muggy. My trailer was like a sweat lodge. The humming little fan in my window seemed almost lethargic in its attempt to combat nature's brazier. It could have been a bee fanning its queen. The leaves of the grasses and trees seemed to droop in the still, moist air. My sodden clothing clung to my skin like marsupial pups. Hours crept around the clock as slowly as the mercury crept up the tube. Beetles and grasshoppers sang arid little ditties, seemingly the only creatures adapted to the heat wave. Inside was hot, outside was hotter, not the hint of a breeze in either location.

How I do wax on. Get to the point, you urge.

Well, it was a distant, barely perceptible rumble that drew me to the door. It could have been a lofty jet or a Harley on the Cains River Road, a grumbling hog. I hoped it was thunder. It was. I saw the anvil on the horizon. The head of a nuclear-like mushroom billowing from ominous blue. I watched it approach for the longest time. Slowly it pushed the sky away. The sun and the afternoon moon slid behind its drapes, gave the storm its day. It was full of greed and wrath and fury; even the air chose to escape. It cooled my skin as it sought refuge in the trees, hayfields, wherever the wind goes. And the storm celebrated each victory, every occupation with fireworks and drums. I stood there and watched and listened; I could not leave the door.

I've watched storms go by to the north or south, in various directions, but rarely have I seen one come straight at me. It was like I was in a gigantic bed and was pulling a huge, cool comforter over me.

I have cosmos planted in a tear-drop patch between my trailer and the shore, and it was upon one of those, the vermilion one on the far end, that the first drop of rain alit. Cooled and refreshed, the blossom bowed in gratitude. The lightning flashed, the thunder bellowed, and the rain, so fertile, multiplied so quickly, became so congested I could barely see the river. It sounded like — and could very well have been — applause.

O! What a feeling! What a relief!

I think every imp and demon on the river took refuge in my trailer, for that's where I lost control. I kicked off my sandals, dropped my pants and shorts, and God help me, not caring about reputation, society, the establishment, the mayor, not caring about what anybody might think of me, I threw caution to the wind and ran naked in the rain.

* Log *

August 4

8:16 A.M. One salmon. 12 pounds. Caught by Nean Kooglin's sport, Donald Jeffries, in the Home Pool behind the Furlong Rock.

9:17 A.M. One grilse. 4 pounds. Caught by Lindon Tucker's sport, Paul Gray, in the Home Pool behind Aunt Sally's Rock.

8:23 P.M. One salmon. 25 pounds. Caught by Cavender Bill in the Home Pool behind the Furlong Rock.

Luther Corhern

The Name Game

I don't know what I'm talking about half the time. Give me a few drinks, however, and you'd think to hear me postulating that I know everything there is to know. Pour me a few more and you'd think I was old Goethe.

Lotty's just as bad. Actually, I think Lotty's worse. She has the ability to rant and rave and sound totally legitimate. Of course, she has legitimate backing. She studied sociology at St. Thomas University. She has the jargon to back her up. Everyone who knows anything is aware there's a lot more to sociology than jargon. I mean, there's . . . ah . . . well, there's normal behaviour and deviant behaviour . . . and who can possibly argue with anyone who knows the word *interaction*. And get a hold of this: one night I was having a little argument with Lotty about my need to better myself, to give my family name more respect. Lotty said, "The trouble with you, Lute, you're a victim of intergenerational social mobility."

"Oh," I said. "No wonder."

I don't think she had a clue what she was talking about, but a mouthful like *intergenerational social mobility* sure shut me up in a hurry.

The answer to winning arguments, to being socially accepted and respected, to being successful in just about every way is to become an authority on one single thing and talk about nothing else. Preachers are great at playing that game. I'm convinced every individual should have a title. No matter what you do, whether you're a wood cutter, a cleaner, a babysitter, or a guide, or whether you do nothing at all, there should be an impressive word to describe the job. Some janitors call themselves sanitational engineers. Pretty impressive. Not a bad handle at all.

"What do you do?" I sweep floors? Doesn't grab ya. Toilet bowl cleaner? Won't do, sounds like you're sniffing too many chemicals. I'm a dust remover? Might as well call yourself a rag or a whisk.

"What do you do?"

"I'm a rag."

"Do you have an opinion on the world problems of today, rag?"

"No, I'm just a rag."

"Any opinions on the world problems of today, Mr. Sanitational Engineer?"

"Of course. We need to polish our act, clean up the environment, mop up crime. We need more sterilization, more ethnic cleansing . . ."

Who's responsible for handing out the titles? Do we do it ourselves? When do cooks start calling themselves chefs? How many pictures do you paint before you start calling yourself an artist? How long do you drive a tractor before you're a heavy equipment operator? If you pound nails, you get to call yourself a carpenter's assistant. Peel potatoes and you're a sous-chef. A sot might call himself a wine taster.

I picked up a hitchhiker the other day. I'd been over to Fredericton and was on my way home, and there he was, standing in the rain. He was a young man, no more than twenty, looked decent, presentable, not too dangerous. I stopped.

"Man!" he said. "Thanks for stopping! That rain is cold!" I noticed he was French.

"My pleasure," I said and turned up the heat. "Where ya heading?"

"Baie Ste. Anne."

"Well, I'm not going that far, but I'll get you half the way. Coming from Fredericton?"

"Yeah. I'm taking a few summer classes at the University of New Brunswick."

"Good for you! What are you studying?"

He rattled off three or four words like science and telekinesis, with an ology here and an ography there, threw in a few bios and subs. I had no idea what he was talking about.

"That's good," I said. "Sounds interesting."

"What do you do?" he asked.

What do I do? What do I do? I'm a guide, of course. But there had to be a better word for it. I wished I'd had a thesaurus with me, I could have come up with a handle like pilotologist for the salmo salar, or fluviographer. But "I'm a guide" was the best I could manage.

What do you do? My sister was a wife and mother for a while. A wife and mother looks after a family, does just about everything. A wife and mother deserves many elegant titles, but everywhere my sister went, people would ask her, "What do you do?"

"I'm a wife and mother," she told them.

"Oh really, how nice, ho-hum," they'd say.

As part of her wife and mother thing, my sister took quite a few snaps of her kids. So one night at a party she was asked the question and she said, "I'm a photographer."

"Oh, really! How wonderful! Freelance?"

"Oh, yes. Yep. Freelance photographer. That's me."

Ever since I picked that guy up on the road, I've thought about it. River tour co-ordinator. Salmon fishing strategist. How would "I'm a rod and reel man" sound at the Lieutenant-Governor's levy?

It's all about status, right? Nobody will walk up to you and ask you if you're smart or stupid, or if you're educated or not.

They simply ask you what you do. Nean, Elvis, Lindon, Stan, Kid, all of us are guides. What we do depends on who we guide. A sport checked into the Salmon Camp a couple of years back and told Cavender Bill, "I'm a non-resident, so I'll be needing a guide. I know where to fish and how to fish, so it doesn't matter who I get — a dummy with a badge will do."

Cavender Bill turned to me.

That was good for the old ego, I tell ya.

Well, you can't let little things like that bother you for very long. It seems to me, if you're a doctor or a lawyer or an Indian chief, you might find yourself constantly living up to your name. Unless, of course, you're really high up in the world, like a prince or a duke, a count or even a king. Then you do whatever comes into your head or nothing at all. I'm a guide, and as long as I'm on the right end of the canoe on a windy day, it's a decent handle.

* Log *

August 25

The fishing still leaves much to be desired. Nean hooked a grilse yesterday and that's the most action we've seen in a long while.

Luther Corhern

The Whitewall Rapids

My uncle used to sit with a straight face and tell me a story about three men going down the river on a marble slab. It was an outrageously funny yarn, but he told it with so much sincerity, with so much conviction that I found myself wanting to believe him.

He was a very good liar, I guess.

I'm not so good at it. When I don't know whether to lie or not, I sort of hem and haw and say things like, "Could be, maybe, I ain't sure, some say yes, some say no," stuff like that. It keeps me looking ignorant, and most ignorant people have friends all over the place. People generally like you if you're ignorant because they can tell you all kinds of stuff they figure you don't know. I think it was Thomas Gray who said, "Where ignorance is bliss 'tis folly to be wise." I don't know more than that one line of Mr. Gray's, but many of us guides here on the Miramichi River sort of take that as our motto. Of course, there's always some lad enters our blissful lives and screws everything all up by telling us something.

But sometimes you can't help thinking you should have said more about the few things you do know. I have that feeling right now. I'm feeling a bit guilty. Yes, I think I should've said more. The trouble is, I was caught in the middle. On one hand was my boss, Cavender Bill, and on the other hand was my friend, Kid Lauder, a guy I grew up with. And it all happened over a salmon pool, which wasn't really a pool at all, and me catching a salmon in it for no other reason than that it was late in the fall, and in the fall, when the salmon are horny and ornery, you can catch one just about any place at all that has water running through it.

Cavender Bill's little outfitting business is doing pretty good. Last season, he must have had forty or fifty guests, and about half of them left happy. That's not bad, considering most of them were Americans and a great many of them had never fished salmon before in their lives.

In July, the fishing got real hard because of the heat, and Cav, being the honest sort, picked up the phone and told the Henderson party from Milwaukee not to bother coming.

"We'll go up anyway," said Mr. Henderson. "It can't be all that bad."

This come-anyway attitude is not unusual. Many Americans think that because they're coming to Canada, the fishing's got to be good, that we're like the Arctic, so, relatively speaking, even if the fishing's not that great according to us, it's gotta be pretty good according to them.

The fact of the matter is, in June, July, and August, here on the Miramichi, the old mercury shoots up to around ninety degrees, and unless we get lots of rain, the salmon are more stand-offish than the Queen of England in a Quebec row. You can never guarantee good fishing except for late in the fall, and even then, you have to say things like, "Could be, maybe, I ain't sure, some say yes, some say no . . ." I'm only a guide, not a god, I'm not old Poseidon.

Anyway, it was late in the fall, coming along toward the end of the season, when Cavender Bill called me into the camp and said, "Lute, I was thinking we're a little short of fishing space, and before I go back home to the States for the winter, I think I'd like to buy another salmon pool."

"Good, good, good," I replied. "Got anything in mind?"

"Well," he said, "I was thinking we need something quite different from what we have already. A high water pool, perhaps."

"Good, good, good. Got anything in mind?"

"What do you think of Kid Lauder's pool? He wants to sell it, you know. Know anything about it? Is it any good?"

"Ah . . . could be, maybe, I ain't sure, some say yes, some say no . . ."

"What d'ya say we go and take a look at it, give it a try."

And that's why I'm feeling guilty. I didn't say anything more than, "Good, good, good," and up to Kid's we went. I already knew what Kid's pool looked like, and I should've told Cav about the car tires, but I didn't. Cavender wanted a pool and Kid wanted more money, and I didn't want to get caught in between. And to tell you the truth, I didn't think we'd catch any fish in it, and Cavender would end up not being interested.

Well, Kid Lauder must have been waltzing with old Poseidon that day, because I stepped into the water, made a long cast right out over the biggest truck tire in the pool, and hooked into what must have been a twenty-pounder. Cavender Bill was so happy with that little occurrence that he didn't even bother fishing the pool himself. He was standing on the shore with Kid, and they shook hands on the deal right then and there.

It wasn't until just the other day that Cav found out the truth of the matter, and he said to me, "Why didn't you tell me that Kid Lauder was a wheeler dealer, Lute?"

Yes, yes, yes . . . I know, I know, I know . . . I should have said more.

You see, about ten or twelve years ago, Kid and his nephew, Corry, got into the real estate business, or the truck tire business, or maybe both. "So what's wrong with that?" you might be asking. Well, I'm not sure, except I very much doubt that Cavender Bill would have paid the big bucks for Kid's pool had he known the truth.

About ten or twelve years ago, Kid Lauder was the proud owner of one of the poorest salmon pools on the Miramichi River. It was a great big flat lake-like stretch of slow-moving water that no salmon in his right mind would even consider holding in. There were swamps on both sides of the river, and the banks were steep with grass and brambles. It was impossible to get any kind of a vehicle to, and, as a matter of fact, even when walking, you'd sink ankle-deep in mud with every step. In other words, the pool wasn't and probably still isn't worth two cents to anybody.

Now, anyone with an ounce of sense would know that the pool needed rocks, big rocks, and lots of them. You can make a pool, no trouble at all, out of any chub hole, even out of a pond like Kid's, if you add enough rocks. However, the trouble with Kid's place was that it was impossible to get your truck loads of rocks to the site. You might drift the rocks downstream on a raft, but that would be too much work, you'd have to build a hundred rafts. It would cost you an arm and a leg, more than the pool would ever be worth.

So Kid came up with an idea.

Tires.

He had about fifty of his own in his junk shed, and the rest he borrowed, found, bought, or stole. He cleaned out everybody's garage and shed from Doaktown to Renous. Truck tires, car tires, tractor tires, tires from Mack semis, Ford Rangers, baby Austins, and utility trailers. He even came and asked me for my old bald Michelin whitewalls — the ones I keep just to look at as a reminder of the good old days when I used to spin the bejesus out of them with that old 1965 327 Biscayne. He even went to Shirley Ramsey and asked her for the ones she'd painted white and was using for planters on her lawn and culvert ends where her driveway meets the road. Every day for about a month, Kid and Corry could be seen pushing those old tires across the field, through the swamp, and over the hill to the river. And once there, they figured out where they wanted to place them, filled them with fist-sized stones from the bottom of the river, and sank them. Presto! His rock, his turbulence, his salmon hold! You see, every time they sank a tire, it picked up the current a bit and created a little indentation on the surface, and pretty soon it even started to *look* like a pool. And after about a month, it began to look like not just any pool, but a pretty good pool. To stand on the hill and look out over the water, you'd think you were gazing upon the choice pool at Wilson's Camps. It looked good enough to fool most Americans, anyway. It fooled Cavender Bill, and he's been coming up here for years.

It wasn't a complete rip-off. You can catch a salmon there if you flail the water long enough or fish it late in the fall. But you can catch a salmon in the Bergen Eddy if you flail the water long enough or fish it late in the fall.

But I suppose I should've told Cav.

Cav's not completely annoyed about it, though. He's got more money than he could ever spend, so whatever he paid for it didn't bother him. As a matter of fact, he and I had quite a laugh over it.

Cav said to me, "Why didn't you tell me Kid Lauder was a wheeler dealer, Lute?"

"Because I never thought of him as a wheeler dealer before," I answered. "But you're right. He sure is!"

"You know, Luther, I remember years ago, back home in Texas, a few of us boys used to frequent a bar that had a rubber rail to put your feet on instead of a brass one. We used to joke about feeling obliged to wear brass-toed boots there. Do you reckon we might need to wear waders made of stone in this new pool of ours?"

"Either that, or fish it from a marble dinghy," I said.

Cav named his new water "The Firestone Pool," and that gave us a bit of a snicker, too. We'll be fishing it in the late fall, no doubt. It's always nice to have a change of scenery.

* Log *

September 9

8:15 A.M. One salmon. 12 pounds. Caught by Cavender Bill in the Home Pool behind the Bellyview Rock.

8:20 A.M. One grilse. 4 pounds. Caught by Lindon Tucker's sport, Ken Vincent, in the Home Pool behind the Furlong Rock.

8:45 A.M. One grilse. 4 pounds. Caught by Nean Kooglin's sport, Harry Wright, in the Home Pool behind the Bellyview Rock.

9:18 A.M. One salmon. 22 Pounds. Caught by Cavender Bill in the Home Pool behind Aunt Sally's Rock.

9:23 A.M. One salmon. 15 pounds. Caught by Elvis Glasby's sport, Herman Thurston, in the Home Pool behind the Furlong Rock.

9:40 A.M. One salmon. 10 pounds. Caught by Lindon Tucker's sport, Ken Vincent, in the Home Pool behind the Bellyview Rock.

10:00 A.M. One grilse. 5 pounds. Caught by Cavender Bill in the Home Pool behind the Furlong Rock.

11:25 A.M. One salmon. 10 pounds. Caught by Nean Kooglin's sport, Harry Wright, in the Home Pool behind Aunt Sally's Rock.

7:20 P.M. One salmon. 15 pounds. Caught by Elvis Glasby's sport, Herman Thurston, in the Home Pool behind the Bellyview Rock.

All today's fish were taken on either Green Machines or Red Butt Butterflies.

Luther Corhern

Moving Right Along

It's important to do things methodically, in an organized fashion. I learned that a long time ago, when I first started guiding for a living. There's nothing worse, or at the very least embarrassing, to be twenty or thirty miles up a wilderness river and find you've forgotten things, a can opener, a sleeping bag, your fishing vest with just about everything you need for successful fishing in it, or some other important item.

Every time I have a busy and important day coming up, I sit at my kitchen table the night before and write a things-to-do list. I did that on Monday night because my cousin Henry and his wife, Jane, were flying in from Toronto at seven o'clock on Tuesday, and I'd told them I'd pick them up at the airport in Fredericton. The plan was that they'd stay with me on the Miramichi on Tuesday night and head up to Campbellton on Wednesday to be with her folks. My trailer was in its usual messy state, I needed groceries and beer, I needed to get a new tire put on the pickup before heading out to Fredericton, it seemed I had a million things to do.

My list read: shower, make coffee, eat breakfast, wash dishes, put garbage out, vacuum living room, scrub kitchen, remove golf clubs and fishing gear from spare room and put in shed, change bedding in spare room, do laundry, go to grocery store, go to liquor store, go to drug store for candles, go to service station for new tire — the list went on and on. When I finished that list, I wrote another one, a grocery list.

As sure as my name is Luther Corhern, I left both lists on the kitchen table. On Tuesday, to get the jump on everything, I got out of bed an hour early and went to the table to check my lists.

They weren't there.

"I'm getting forgetful," I thought. "I must have put them somewhere else."

I checked the fridge door, the cupboards, the coffee table, the book shelves, the dresser in the bedroom, the floor underneath the table . . . I looked for the darn things for an hour. So much for rising early. I still haven't found them.

But everything was all right, I started the day without them, and I think I covered everything on the one having to do with household chores.

"Now I need to go to Miramichi," I thought. "I need to write another grocery list." It took me ten or fifteen minutes, but that was okay, things were moving along.

It was on my way to Miramichi that I remembered I needed a new tire. That tidbit of information came to me when the one on the pickup went flat. I had a spare, but it took me fifteen or twenty minutes to make the change. I was still moving along.

I went to the grocery store and picked up everything on my new list. There were five cash registers in the store, two of which were open. I approached the shortest line. Only four people ahead of me. The first person had enough groceries in his cart to feed a family for a month, I figured. The cashier rang everything in swiftly, however, and that left three.

The next person had only a few things but got in an argument with the cashier about the price of a pound of bacon. "It's on sale," she said. "You rang in $3.25 for that and I'm sure the tag read $2.95. What gives?"

"This is President's Choice bacon. Simon's is on sale. See?"

"I didn't look at that little tag. I was talking about the one back at the refrigerators."

"I'll page Sam. Sam to the number two, please. Sam to number two."

It took Sam about five minutes to respond. They discussed the issue, Sam went back to the refrigerators, returned in about five more minutes with a pound of Simon's $2.95 bacon for the lady.

"But I don't want Simon's. I want President's Choice. Ring it in. I'll pay the extra thirty cents."

"Thank God," I whispered.

The next person in the line-up made it through quickly. The lady directly ahead of me spent five minutes finding seventy-eight cents change in her massive purse. Then it was my turn. Frustrated but happy that I was finally there, I placed my items in front of the cashier with a sigh. "I'll not complain about anything," I told myself. "I'm running out of time. I don't care about a few cents here or there." I had a pretty good idea how much my things would cost, so I had my money ready. The cashier rang in the bacon and eggs, the bread and beans, the mushrooms and plums. That's when the ribbon in the cash register ran out. Ten minutes later, I paid for my $27.69 worth of groceries and left the store. I had shopped for five minutes and spent twenty-five at the cash register.

In the liquor store line-up, the bottleneck was much more trendy: instead of change-counters and complainers, half the folks ahead of me paid for their pleasure with a bank card. Now, the bank card is a piece of plastic that people with money in the bank use when they don't have money in their pockets. Then everyone else has to wait for a computer to vouch for the fact that they do have money in the bank. The computer spits out a slip of paper that the guy with the empty wallet signs. Some have cards for just about every bank in existence, but still they don't seem to know which bank has enough money in it to cover a bottle of Lamb's Navy Rum. There was a run of these that day, and several ended up fishing out their wallets and paying with real money anyway.

Two minutes shopping, ten minutes in the line-up, sighing, shuffling my feet, waiting to see if other people's banks would give them the price of a bottle.

At the drug store, I picked up six long white candles and six short red ones. When the cashier scanned the white ones, everything worked fine. But when the computer couldn't or wouldn't read the short red ones, the cashier paged a supervisor, and, as if he thought the cashier was stupid, he tried scanning them. No go, of course, so he went back to the candle shelf for some others he thought might work. When that failed, he did what he should have done in the first place: rang in a number, punched the six button, and the computer said, "Thank you very much, that will be $10.95." I paid for the candles, and, much to the delight of the ten people waiting behind me, I got out of there.

Running about an hour behind at this point, I went to the service station for a new tire. There were about eight guys standing around, three of whom were working. None of them acknowledged me, no Hello, may I help you, not as much as a nod.

"Ahem," I went.

No response.

"Ahem!" I tried once again.

Nothing.

Maybe they're all customers, I thought. Maybe they're all deaf and blind. Maybe I dropped dead in the liquor store and I'm really not here at all.

Finally a guy came through a door, spotted me, and asked, "What can I do for ya?"

"I need a new tire. I need that old one removed from the rim and the new one put on."

The guy checked his watch. "Yep," he said. "We can do that for ya in about an hour."

"An hour?"

"We're running a little behind here."

"You, too, eh?"

"What's that?"

"Nothing."

In the end, I thought I'd make up time by driving fast to the Fredericton airport. Over there where the road follows the Nashwaak River, where it's as crooked as a snake's path and there's about ten miles of double line, I pulled up behind an old man with a hat. It doesn't matter where I go, I get behind the same old man with a hat. You probably know him, he's oblivious to everybody and everything but his pipe and the weather forecast on the radio. I got behind him again on the Lincoln Road that leads to the airport. Didn't matter, though, because the cops had a roadblock set up. One of them took ten minutes to fine me $84.00 for not renewing my registration in time.

I was an hour and a half late getting to the airport. I sensed Henry and Jane were ready to strangle me.

"Where were you?" asked Jane. "We were about ready give up on you, to hire a cab!"

"I'm sorry," I said. "I had a bad day, had a million things to do. And then I had a flat tire and then got stopped by the cops . . ."

"Know what I do when I have a day like that, Luther? I make a list, write everything down. I find it helps."

"I must try to remember to do that, Jane," I said.

"Well, no harm done," said Henry. "We couldn't have hired a cab, anyway."

"How come?" I asked.

"I don't know. My damn bank card wouldn't work in that stupid machine!"

"Well, that's the way it goes. Welcome. You're here!"

"Yep. Great world, eh? Just a few hours ago, we were in Toronto."

"Yes, sir," I agreed. "That's life in the fast lane."

* Log *

October 15

Last day of the season.

Didn't fish. Went to the airport.

Luther Corhern

Winning the Lottery

Wealth is a peculiar and confusing concept. I have very little understanding of it, of course, being a humble guide and logger. My knowledge about being rich is limited to what I've read and the things I've seen on television — big houses and cars, fine clothes and jewellery, exotic food and drink, power. I've dreamed about being rich, but I pay no attention to dreams. I figure that my subconscious mind knows as little or maybe even less about the concept than my visible, awake, touchable, here-and-now, conscious state does, that is if the subconscious is where dreams come from. It seems to me that there are more people pretending to be rich than there are actual rich people. If a man lives in a million-dollar house and owes for most of it, is he any richer than the man who lives in a paid-for hut? Are you not the equivalent of a millionaire if you have a possession that you wouldn't sell for a million dollars?

Most people don't realize how rich they are until they see somebody much poorer, a starving and homeless child in some third world country. I've seen the super rich and the extremely poor on television, and one's as hard for me to comprehend as the other. When you look at either end of the scale, your own concept of wealth and poverty becomes rather meaningless.

When I was a child, my daddy was a farmer, a lumberjack, a guide, a seasonal worker. In the spring he'd till the soil with horse and plow, and I'd run along behind with a bean can collecting worms for fishing, the north-bound Canada geese honking high above, the first robin of the year serenading us from a nearby chokecherry bush. Seeing the geese, hearing the robin, finding the plump worms for my hook made me feel wealthy. And in the summer I felt wealthy when the seeds my father planted became actual carrots and turnips, lettuce, beets, and corn, and the robin's chosen bush was laden with ripened chokecherries. I felt rich in the autumn when the bins were full of vegetables enough to last the winter and when my father came home from a successful hunt. I remember feeling rich when my father got a job skirting the Howard Road, had a steady income for a great deal of the winter. A steady income! Now that was wealth! I felt rich, too, when my mother performed her magic in the kitchen, the loaves, the roasts, stews, cakes, and pies.

I didn't always feel rich, of course. In late October and November, that season between seasons when the south-bound geese foretold winter, the honking, the same honking that seemed gay in the spring, now sounded lonesome and forlorn, and the ensuing silence sometimes left me in a state of melancholy, feeling desolate, poor, and on the verge of tears.

I once watched a play about poor peasants who spent much of their time discussing a mysterious lottery. They had all put their names in a hat and were waiting for the big moment, the draw. When the draw finally occurred, the winner turned out to be the loser, the winner was to be sacrificed to the gods or something. It seems to me that the name drawn belonged to a young girl, a virgin, and the rest of the community carried out the sacrifice by stoning her to death.

I sometimes wonder if winning a few million dollars would be equally lethal. I love scotch, food, sex, gambling, fishing, golfing, and travelling, a pretty lethal mixture for a man with a million dollars. Oh, I also love to give and share, to watch the sun rise and set, to make people feel good, to see smiles and hear laughter, to entertain people with my old guitar, but basically I think I'd be a roué if I could afford it.

The other night Nean, Lindon, Elvis, Buck, and I went to

the Devil's Elbow on Cains River to toast the river and the salmon, our annual post-season celebration of the great outdoors we all love so much. Along about dark someone asked, "What would you do if you won a million dollars?"

"If I had a million dollars," said Elvis, "I'd buy a nice comfortable home and a pink Cadillac. Then I'd lay right back and take 'er easy. I'd have a couple of Thai virgins doing the cooking and cleaning for me and a Caterpillar bulldozer the size of a German tank just to make snow removal a bit more interesting in the winter."

"I'd get myself a new fishing rod," said Lindon. "A new fishing rod, yeah. An eight, no, a nine, maybe a ten-footer with a, with a, with a, oh, I don't know, with a, maybe a new Cortland 444 and an English reel. New waders, too, and a new vest, and about ten fly boxes all full of nice new Cossebooms and Green Machines, most of them all shiny and, and, and . . . oh, boys, I tell ya . . ." Lindon slid into a fantasy and sat dreamily for a while, thinking, I supposed, about the ten-footer.

"Me?" said Buck. "I'd like to have one of those satellite dishes that brings you in about a hundred channels and a television with a screen about the size of a barn door. Of course, I'd have to build on a room to put it in. A new set of golf clubs wouldn't be bad either. How about you, Lute?"

I had been thinking of scotch, food, sex, travelling. "Oh, me? I don't know. I think a lad would have to have a bit of a party, you know, treat his friends. I wouldn't mind having a new four-wheel drive. But, what about helping the poor? It seems to me that a lad's soul could do with a bit of giving."

"Well, yeah."

"Sure, we'd have to give a little."

"Yeah, you know, to the church and stuff like that."

Lindon snapped out of his dreams. "Yes! Of course! Aha.

Give, yeah. Invest in some good fly tying material, tie your own flies, and give a few away. 'Go ahead,' I'd say. 'Take that nice Butterfly there, the one with the red butt, and take a few of them Green Machines while you're at it.' Oh, yes, give, for sure."

"I was referring to giving to the poor, the hungry, the disabled, the artists."

"Yeah, well, I'd give the odd salmon away, you know, if the fishing was good."

"How much you gave away would have to do with how much money you won on the lottery," said Buck. "Now, if I won a lot of money, I'd make sure that every kid had a television. If I won a million, I'd give them seventeen-inch screens. If I won several million, I'd give them twenty-inch screens. It's all relative."

"You watch a lot of TV, don't you?"

"Not much else to do, in the winter anyway."

"I was hitchhiking once," put in Elvis. "This lad picked me up and drove me all the way home, went twenty miles out of his way. I always remembered it. Good thing for him to do. I'd do that if I was rich. I'd drive someone home if I had a pink Cadillac and could afford the gas to put in it."

"You're a wonderful lot," I said.

"What would you do, Lute? Throw a party? What else?"

"I don't know, pay bills, give to the poor, I don't know. It's all just a dream for us guys anyway."

"What about investing?" asked Nean. "Maybe set your friends up in business or something, buy into IBM or smokeless tobacco or whatever."

"Me, now, I'd invest in a salmon pool," said Lindon. "I'd buy the best damn pool on the Miramichi River, fish it every day all summer long, and give half the fish to the priest. Keep him fatter than old Friar Tuck."

"I'd buy a million acres of forest," said Nean. "I'd put a twelve foot fence around it and not allow a human being to enter. A sanctuary, I'd call it. No hunters or lumberjacks allowed. That'd be good for the world, wouldn't it?"

One thing I noticed, the longer we talked, the more serious the conversation grew. Before we quit, we were actually arguing about money. Nean accused Elvis of not paying him back twenty dollars.

"I don't owe you twenty dollars," said Elvis.

"You do so! I loaned you a twenty after the Legion closed one night last winter. You wanted to buy a case of beer. Remember?"

"Yeah, but you drank half of it!"

"Yeah, well, then, you owe me ten dollars!"

"I do not! Cheapskate!"

When that argument finally died down, Lindon confronted me about why I didn't buy my flies from him. "You don't tie your own and you don't buy them from me," he said. "Where do you get them?"

"I go to a store where they have thousands," I said. "That way I can look a bunch of them over and pick out the ones I want. You only have a few, and sometimes they're not all that great."

"Yeah, well, thanks a lot, buddy buddy, pal! See if I get you to make any paddles for me!"

Something was going wrong and I knew it. I've heard it said, the richer your friends, the more they cost you. I'm inclined to wonder if rich people have any friends at all. If Buck, the old TV watcher, hadn't stepped in and lightened things up, I think we'd have been enemies before we left the Devil's Elbow that night. He hadn't been paying much attention to our arguments, so he came out with something that we all couldn't help but agree on.

He said, "You know that show that's on in the morning? *Breakfast Television?*"

We all stopped our arguing and looked at him.

"Yes," said Elvis. "What about it?"

"Well, I was just thinking, if I won the lottery, I'd go out and buy their poor cameramen some tripods."

No arguments there. As a matter of fact, we had a good laugh about it.

And then, from somewhere up above, we heard the geese honking and chatting in broken voices not unlike a group of adolescent boys. The southbound Canada geese, richer and freer than any man on Earth.

I stopped to listen.

The melancholy curtain dropped.

I was at the Devil's Elbow on the beautiful Cains River and one moment I was discussing money, feeling rich, and laughing, and the next moment I felt so very poor, knowing that I would not be there for long.

That's life, I guess.

* Log *

October 31

Halloween. The salmon fishing season is closed, so nothing much is happening. A few of the boys are gearing up for the hunting season, and that's about all. Cavender Bill has gone back to Texas, but before he left, and I'm not sure why, he asked me to continue writing in this log. I don't mind. It gives me something to do.

Luther Corhern

A One-Horse Hope
and Sleigh, Eh?

It snowed a little bit this morning. Barely enough to cover the ground, but it stayed. Not much heat in the sun when a mere dust sticks around for the whole day like that.

It's funny, and it might not sound very Canadian, but of all the things nature has to throw at me, I dislike snow the most.

But that first storm?

I don't know, I must admit, I sort of like it. It's winter's equivalent to April showers, I guess. April showers green up the grass, the first snowfall masks the expressionless face of early winter.

Many years ago, a gigantic star shone in the eastern sky, showed three wise men where to go, then the sky clouded over and the first snowfall of the year came down. It fell gently on everything from Peruvian temples to Mars Hill olives, from Japanese rice fields to Douglas firs. It fell on ice-covered rivers, effectively shutting down the lights for the salmon below. It snowed all over the world. The first snowfall of the year carries the spirit of Christmas on its wings to this very day.

Today, when it began to snow, without even thinking, I opened the closet door and fished out the Christmas trimmings. I put the face of Santa in the window, strung lights around the door. I decorated the juniper tree out front with the tops of the bean, soup, and Irish stew cans I'd been saving all year for that purpose. At night, the can tops reflect the lights around the door and become the prettiest things you ever laid your eyes on. Two hundred yards away, from out on the Hemlock Road, the juniper takes on the appearance of a little star tree.

While I worked, I whistled "Jingle Bells." I believe "Jingle Bells" was written by a Canadian.

> *Jingle bells, jingle bells, jingle all the way,*
> *Oh, what fun it is to ride in a one horse open sleigh, eh?*

All the time I was growing up, I never knew what a one horse open sleigh was. I thought the words of the song went, "Oh, what fun it is to ride in a one horse hope and sleigh." And, of course, I didn't quite know what a "one horse hope" might be, either.

My friend Nean Kooglin is quite a singer. He likes that song, "Love Potion Number Nine." He sings:

> *I took my troubles down to Madame Roo,*
> *You know that Gypsy with the gold tattoo . . .*

When I told him the Gypsy's name was Ruth and that she had a gold-capped tooth, he shrugged and admitted that he'd been singing it wrong, but I've noticed he still sings it the same old way. Nean always had a soft spot in his heart for women with tattoos.

The big flakes came down on open wings, slowly, as if attached to parachutes. They reminded me of the flakes that alit on Perry Como's white jacket and never melted.

Anyway, while I was trimming the juniper and wondering why Bing Crosby never wore gumshoes in the snow, Ken Hunter came out of the flurries, dressed for winter — his Mackinaw bespeckled with flakes, a nylon stocking pulled over his head to keep his ears warm. Ken's a tall, dark-haired man who always has that aura of too much hard work about him. Another thing about him is that he never says hello or goodbye. He just sort of comes and goes, like a cat or a dog.

This morning, he just walked up to me and said, "Old Charlie Hanson used to drink his rum from a pigskin pouch. Just spurted it straight into his mouth, like water or juice or something."

"How's she goin', Ken?"

"Interested in buying a Christmas tree?" he asked. I guess the little snowfall had started him thinking about Christmas, too.

"How much you asking?"

"Three dollars a foot."

"What kind of tree is it?"

"What else. Bammy balsam."

"Fir, eh?"

"I got a nice eight-footer for ya, Lute. I can deliver it to ya this afternoon."

"A Christmas tree, eh. Well, let's see, now . . . my mobile home has an eight-foot ceiling . . . I'd have to make room for a stand at the bottom and I have a star for the top . . . I'd need a six-and-a-half- or seven-foot tree."

"Well, you could always cut a foot off the bottom."

"Or maybe you could cut it off, and I could pay you for a seven-footer instead of an eight."

"Well, it's a pretty tree. I'd hate to be the one to have to cut it off like that."

"For an eight-foot tree, you're talking twenty-four dollars. Right?"

"Yep. Three dollars a foot."

"So you want me to pay you for an eight-foot tree, when I only need a seven. I get to pay you three extra dollars for the privilege of cutting it back a foot myself."

"But it's the prettiest tree I've got. It would be a shame to cut it off."

"So sell me a smaller tree."

"You like having a pretty tree, right?"

"Well, of course."

"Then this is the tree for you."

"But I'd have to cut it off to stand it in the house, and then it wouldn't be so pretty," I reasoned.

"It's up to you what you do with it," he said.

Christmas is about giving, and Ken Hunter has a wife and three small children. He guides occasionally and works in the woods when he can find a job. I knew he needed the money. However, I was not about to pay twenty-four dollars for an eight-foot tree when all I needed was a seven-footer. So I bickered, took advantage of his poverty, I suppose, and finally beat him down to twenty-one dollars.

"I'll cut it off with care," I told him. "A little from the top and a little from the bottom."

"You drive a hard bargain, Lute, but it's a deal. I'll deliver it this afternoon."

"Okay," I said as he walked away.

After he left, I went inside, made myself a cup of coffee, and sat to ponder the whole thing.

I'd been out there with the spirit of Christmas in my heart, trimming the juniper with the shiny tops of tin cans. Frugal enough exercise, I figured. But all of a sudden, I found myself dishing out twenty-one dollars for a tree that I could have found myself, right back here on my own land. Then I grabbed a pen and paper and began to figure. "Twenty-one dollars for a tree. Some of the lights I have are not working, so I'll need to spend about ten dollars for replacements. Then, there'll be gifts to be bought for Mom and Dad, my brothers and sisters, and their children — a couple of hundred dollars there. I'll spend another fifty to sixty dollars for the extra rum and beer I'll need to treat the boys with. I'll have to drive into Newcastle or Fredericton to do that kind of shopping. Because I don't buy expensive things for people, I should be able to get off with spending four to five hundred dollars by the time Boxing Day rolls around."

That's me. Because I'm not very rich and am basically cheap.

Other people go all out, buy diamond rings and fur coats, throw big parties.

All of a sudden, the whole concept depressed me.

"What have we done to Christmas?" I asked myself. "Decorations all over the place, ads on the radio between every song, people rushing around in the cold trying to find a few more dollars to buy that one last gift, others getting drunk or stoned or both, children brainwashed into believing they deserve expensive toys even if they've been spoiled brats all year. I know some people who even buy gifts for their pets. What's happening here? What have we turned this sacred day into? Would it not be a more fitting celebration of Christianity to give all that money to the poor?

"I don't know. This whole gift-exchanging thing might be the very best of a practice. What do I know? I'm just a fishing guide. People should be more like Lindon Tucker and me. Lindon has no family to spend Christmas with, no one to buy for. So every year he and I exchange gifts. One year I gave him a tie. Because he never wears a tie and kept it like new, he gave it back to me two years later. I suppose he forgot who had given it to him. I think I could save a few bucks by giving it back to him this year."

I was sipping my coffee, trying to hang on to the Christmas spirit. Outside, the snow was still gently falling. For some reason, perhaps because of the barometric pressure, you can almost smell the first snowfall.

"It seems to me," I thought, "that you can spend all the money you want, give something to everyone you know, and have your living room stacked half full of gifts on Christmas morning, but nothing gives you the Christmas spirit more than the first fall of snow. We should name the day the first snow falls Christmas and leave it at that. Well, what can you do? Conglomerates have blazed the trail. We live in a capitalist society. We're trapped. Enough of this old foolish thinking. Get on with life, Lute."

I shrugged the whole matter off and turned on the radio. It's total nonsense for a lad like me to try and change the world.

"Just twenty-four shopping days until Christmas," said the radio announcer. "And our doors are open from eight in the morning until ten at night. Buy now and save! And that brings the time around to twenty-five minutes after the hour of eleven o'clock. And now, here's Bing Crosby with 'Silent Night.'"

I may have been thinking like Scrooge, but I love that old carol. It's my favourite, I think. It makes me feel kind of warm inside. I went to the window. The snow had stopped already, as if my humbug attitude had turned everything off. The Christmas spirit was still with me, however, and I started singing along with old Bing.

> *Silent night, holy night,*
> *All is calm, all is bright.*
> *Round John Virgin, mother and child . . .*

Luther Corhern

On Sabbatical

Here on the Miramichi, we have a month of spring, five months of summer, a month of autumn and about five months of winter. But the time from the day the first unemployment insurance cheque comes in the middle of November until April 15, when Cavender Bill opens up the Salmon Camp for black salmon fishing, seems more like a year than five months. I think it's the long nights that make the winter last forever. In mid-winter, the sun goes to bed any time after four o'clock in the day and doesn't rise from its den until eight the next morning. Even when it's up, it just seems to peep at us from behind the southern horizon. Nean Kooglin mused that the sports take the sun and the geese home to the USA with them every fall.

During winter on the Miramichi, the only way you can get your car started in the morning is to make sure you have a block heater installed and plug it in every time you kill the engine. Last summer, Lindon Tucker was guiding a young lady from down south somewhere, and when she saw all the cars with the plugs dangling from their grills, she commented, "My, my! Aren't you Canadians clever! Driving electric cars!" She thought we were looking after the Miramichi smog problem, I suppose.

Last evening, when I stepped out of my trailer to go to the Legion, the first thing I noticed were the northern lights. They seemed to be whitewashing the sky or diapering the Bear. I watched them dance and flicker, sometimes all the way to the zenith. Some people say they make a noise like static or like the wind. One lad told me he could hear them over the sound of his car engine as he was driving along the road — heard them, didn't know what was making the noise, stopped and got out, and there they were. But I, being a Corhern, could never hear them. A bit of deafness runs in the Corhern family. I never met a Corhern yet that could hear a bird any smaller than a raven.

I could have watched them for hours, but I was in a bit of a hurry — it was nearly seven o'clock and the Chicken Shoot at the Legion starts at seven. So I scraped a bit of frost off the windshield and skeedaddled for the village.

The old truck was a bit sluggish, the roads a bit icy, and damn it! I arrived late. When I rushed into the Legion, bought a beer, and hurried into the dart room, I found they had started the game without me.

"No chicken tonight," I muttered and sat to watch.

A Chicken Shoot is a dart game, a round robin type of contest, and if you win it, you get a chicken. I'm not that great a dart player and probably wouldn't have won anyway, but all the same, I like to play and was a bit disappointed.

"Oh, well," I said to myself. "I guess I'll have to put the evening in drinking beer and being a spectator."

The only other lad that wasn't playing for the coveted chicken was Boiler Washburn, so I figured that, with nothing else to do, I'd have a say with him. Boiler's a big, homely fellow who spends half his time guiding and the other half drinking beer. He has a quick mind and is always good for a joke, so I could do worse than sit out a game with Boiler.

"What've ya been up to, Boiler? Have a good Christmas?"

"Spent 'er on rum, mostly," he said.

"How'd Santa use ya? Did ya get your case of oranges?"

"Yep. I got three cases. I get three cases every year, sure as Christmas rolls around. You?"

"Just got the one this year. But Elvis, I think, got three or four."

"Well, that figures. He did guide a lot o' lads from Florida and them places. I don't even like oranges, do you?"

"Not much."

You see, Boiler, Elvis, Lindon, Nean, and a few more of us guide salmon fishermen from the States, and quite often we guide the same fisherman every year. Well, when you spend a week or two on the river every year with the same sport, you get to know him pretty well, you get to be friends. Now, many of the sports we guide are richer than old Solomon, and when Christmas rolls around, they send us presents. Oranges, generally. We can buy oranges in Blackville or Doaktown, just about anywhere, but, well, I guess those guys from the States don't know that.

"Lindon Tucker got oranges from that fellow he guided from Florida, and he told me they were as big as grapefruits," I commented. "Doing anything these days, Boiler?"

"No, I'm on sabbatical, same as yourself."

Boiler always refers to unemployment insurance as *sabbatical*.

"Lindon got his two thousand, I hear."

"Yep. Two thousand and two. He got three the last day of the season."

"That's good fishin'. I only got six hundred so far."

"Well, Lindon's twenty, thirty years older than you, and he fishes a lot. Six hundred salmon's not bad. Six hundred's not a number anyone can sneeze at, even if you never caught another salmon in your life."

"I'm not complaining."

"Did ya get your moose?"

"No. You?"

"A big, old one, tougher than horse hooves."

"I hear Lorne Dolan's not too good."

"Yeah. Heard that, too."

"Nean told me he's got ferunculosis or somethin' like that, he wasn't sure."

"Hmm. Well, he'll pull through."

Boiler and me talked for an hour or so, but once the beer started to kick in, we changed the topic to something more spicy and intelligent: the best way to salt salmon and gaspereaux. We got into quite an argument about it. Boiler believed that you should make a brine strong enough to float a potato, then put your fish in it. I always just throw salt over the fish and let them make their own brine. Boiler said that leaving the fish to make their own brine takes all the good out of them. We argued over that for about two hours and probably would have ended up in a fight if we hadn't been level-headed adults and shaken hands man-to-man on the compromise that the best way to put a salmon up for the winter is to freeze it.

Just then old George Kennedy was eliminated from the Chicken Shoot. His opponent, Beak Flynn, beat him fair and square by picking off a triple two. Old George was not very happy about losing out on the chicken, I tell ya. You'd think by the way he turned red in the face and made excuses that he had just lost a member of his family. At first, he tried to bend the rules a bit by allowing that you couldn't go out on a triple two, and when that didn't work, he said he'd lost because he had been distracted.

"Well, who in the name of God distracted ya?" asked Nean.

Old George looked about the room, spotted Boiler and me sitting together minding our own business, and pointed his finger at us. "Them two argin', gumshoe-lickin', flap-mouthed ganders over there!" he shouted.

Well, I tell ya, as they say down river, them were fightin' words. At least they would have been fighting words had they come from anyone else other than old George Kennedy, who was about three times older than Boiler and me. Coming from an old man like George, the words just sounded funny, showed that he still had some sand in him.

"Aw, c'mon, George," said Boiler. "We never bothered ya. C'mon over and have a drink with us. C'mon over and we'll buy you a beer or a rum. Buy 'im a drink, Lute."

"Why me?"

"Well, you're the lad that didn't know what he was talkin' about when it comes to saltin' fish!"

I didn't want to get back into that argument again, so I went to the bar and bought old George a drink of rum. He calmed down when he saw me heading for the bar, so I guess it was worth it.

It wasn't long until others started to get beat out, and pretty soon the Chicken Shoot was down to just two fellows, Omer Gaston and Lyman MacFee. Both Omer and Lyman were shooting deadly darts, and all of a sudden, when Lyman still had a hundred and ten left on the board, he shot a twenty, triple twenty, double fifteen. A three dart finish! The game was over.

Amid a big round of applause, Antoine Firlog, the bartender, came from behind the bar and presented the happy Lyman MacFee with a nice, plump, four-pound chicken. When Lyman had gracefully accepted the prize and held it up for all us lads to admire, we gave him another big hand.

"Sometimes it's just as much fun not to play," I commented.

"Yep," said Boiler. "Well, it's time to hit the road. I better go out and start the old truck up, warm 'er a bit."

"Good idea," I said, handing him my keys. "Start mine up while you're at it, will ya?"

I thought I'd let the truck warm up for about fifteen minutes before I hit the road, so I bought myself another beer and was standing at the bar having a say with Antoine when Boiler comes back in, stomps the snow off his feet, and saunters up to the bar.

"Gimme a double rum," he says to Antoine.

"Pretty stiff drink for driving home on, isn't it?" I commented.

"Well, I changed my mind about goin' home," said Boiler. "I thought I'd maybe spend the night with you."

"Me? You'd still have to drive to my place, wouldn't you?"

"Well, that shouldn't be any problem," he says. "You got your trailer parked right outside in the parking lot."

"What d'ya mean, my trailer's outside in the parking lot?"

"Just what I told ya! Your trailer's right outside the Legion in the parkin' lot."

"But . . . ah, darn! I forgot to unplug the pickup again!"

The boys had a pretty good laugh at that, I tell ya.

"That's the very best, Lute, old boy!" says Boiler. "You don't have to worry about cops, driving on icy roads, or anything else! Have yourself another beer!"

Anyway, as far as the log goes, there's not much going on around here these days. We're all just tying a few flies, attending the odd Chicken Shoot, you know, as Boiler says, on sabbatical, putting the winter in.

Luther Corhern

My Inheritance

The other day, when Nean and I were sitting around griping about the hard winter, Nean brings up the subject of inheritance. "If we were to inherit a million dollars, life would be different," he says. "Just think about it. We could be sitting here planning a trip to some tropical climate instead of complaining about the snow. This time next week, we could be sitting on a balcony overlooking the eighteenth green of some classy golf course in Florida or Cuba, watching the breeze play in a palm tree, listening to some colourful, long-tailed bird nestled in the shade muttering about the lack of rain. Any chance of anyone in your family leaving you a million dollars, Lute?"

"Not a chance in the world," I said.

"You never know, Lute. There might be somebody, some relative out there with too much money to spend . . . somebody might be stashing away coins and dollars, and you don't know about it. One day you might get out of bed and find yourself a millionaire. There might be somebody out there, Lute."

I tried to think about who that somebody might be. With the exception of Uncle Tim, all I could envision was little homes in tired fields owned by relatives with more children than you'd care to count. No money, no swimming pools, no big cars. Uncle Tim was the only one with money.

"Uncle Tim's got money, I think," I said to Nean. "And no offspring to give it to. He's all alone as far as I know."

"Well, there you go, Lute. You ought to visit him once in a while, help him out a bit. He's getting up there in years. You never know, he might take a liking to you."

"I imagine there's somebody closer to him than me. How about you, Nean? Any money in your family?"

"Not really. I might get Uncle Joe's old place when he passes on. That old place ain't worth the taxes he pays on it, though."

I've been thinking about that conversation with Nean a bit, and as far as I can see, other than Uncle Tim's money and big noses, there's only three things that we Corherns can expect to inherit: longevity, deafness, and forgetfulness. It's not unusual for a Corhern to live to be a hundred. My great-grandfather lived to be a hundred and three, several of my great-uncles were still breathing God's sweet air as centenarians, and many of my uncles and aunts reached ninety-plus. Today, we may not be as clean living or as wholesome, and we may have been sprayed with DDT as children, but my generation are getting along in years pretty well, too.

I grew up on the Corhern homestead (inherited by my cousin Pluto), which meant that I got to know many of my relatives quite well. They'd come to visit my grandparents and stay sometimes for as much as a week. Ancient, forgetful, deaf, and for the most part happy old men and women. I have fond memories of them. They were the very best of people. One thing I remember is that they all had a great sense of humour. I guess that, too, was a trait of the Corherns.

It was a great experience for me. They'd sit around and argue religion and politics over and over again, forgetting that they'd just had the same argument perhaps as recently as an hour before. They'd open up windows and reveal tidbits from *their* grandfathers' days, but they couldn't remember what happened an hour before. I remember my grandfather singing me a song called "The Donahue Spree," a song that went on and on for twenty-some verses. An hour later he'd say, "Did I ever sing you 'The Donahue Spree'?"

"Yes, Grandfather, you just sang it an hour ago."

"Eh?"

"I said, You just sang it an hour ago!"

"Bah! I never liked that one. I'll sing you 'The Donahue Spree' instead."

Grandfather used to forget that the TV was a TV and carry on the greatest conversations with people like Fred Davis and Bill Robertson, even Lucille Ball. On the news, Bill Robertson would say, "A plane crash claimed the lives of seventeen people this morning near Calcutta . . ."

"Eh? What did you say?" my grandfather would ask.

My great-grandfather would drive his horse ten miles to the village to pick up sugar or yeast, chat with a few of his friends, and return home, forgetting why he went to the village in the first place. When I was a child, I found his pipe in the shed. It had the words "lard" and "tea" etched on it in my great-grand-mother's handwriting.

Names are the first things to escape our minds. People walk up to me all the time and say, "Hi Lute! How ya doin'?" And I have no idea whatsoever who the hell they are. Recently I was talking to a guy I know. Philip Martin. I talked to him for an hour. Shook his hand, patted him on the back, asked about his family, his job, the fishing, his golf game, and called him Alfred all the while. He had a familiar face, you understand. And Alfred was pretty close.

They say you can do certain things to help you remember. Apparently it has to do with your brain. A young lady from Connecticut once told me that diet is important: eat the right foods and your brain will function better. Another thing I heard about is exercise, that you need to exercise your brain in much the same way as you need to exercise the rest of your body. Walking, jogging, swimming and the like are very important, get the old oxygen flowing up there, but physical exercise is not all you need. To help retain your memory, you also need mental exercise. Read, do crossword puzzles, think about things.

While I still have the capacity to remember what I'm doing, I've already started doing crossword puzzles. Every morning I pick up the paper, read the headlines, scan the sports page to see where the Canadiens stand, then go directly to the crossword puzzle. I'm not good at it, I rarely complete one. Crossword puzzles have peculiar words in them, recurring words that always escape my memory. Words like ogee, oleo, etui, and eddas; clues like Greek letter, Michaelmas daisy, and Fido's scrap. But my goal is not to finish the darn things. My goal is to exercise my brain. While I do them, I drink several cups of coffee and smoke seven or eight cigarettes. I'm optimistic that I'll still be the genius I am today when I reach the ripe old age of ninety.

I suppose I'm no different than anyone else. We all inherit the traits of our forebears. I guess I should consider myself lucky that my family history doesn't include tales of rapists and murderers, charlatans and frauds. At least, not in anyone's memory.

I should have known better, but a seed had been planted in my brain, and I couldn't help but think that Nean might have a point, that Uncle Tim might take a liking to me if I paid him a visit. He'd been a truck driver for fifty years, never got married, never had any children, didn't drink or smoke, and never spent a penny that he couldn't account for. "He's getting old," I thought, "and it would be a kind gesture to go and see him. Nothing wrong in going to see the old guy."

Still thinking along these lines, last Monday I picked up a bag of molasses cookies at Stan's Convenient Store and headed down to Uncle Tim's. I knocked five times before he finally came to the door.

"I thought I heard someone knocking," he greeted me,

"and by God I was right. There you are! What are you selling?"

"Nothing. I just came to see you. How have you been?"

"Sea food! I never eat sea food. Now, if you had some nice smelts . . ."

"No, no, Uncle Tim. I'm not selling fish, I'm your nephew Lute. Do you mind if I come in?"

"In. In. Who are ya, anyway?"

"Lute! Luther Corhern! Your nephew!"

"Whose boy are ya?"

"I'm your brother Bill's boy!"

"Bill, you say?"

"Yes, your brother Bill's boy!"

"Bill? I don't owe any bills! And I don't want any fish!"

"I brought you some molasses cookies," I said.

"What?"

"I brought you some molasses cookies!"

"Oh! Why didn't you say? How much?"

"They're yours for free, Uncle Tim. Here. Take them. They're for you."

"Okay. Thanks. See you later. Watch the roads. I imagine they're slippery."

"Yep. Okay. See you later."

So much for that idea. I should have known better. He didn't know who I was. He didn't even remember who my father was.

The other day I met Johnny Washburn in the mall, and he told me a joke. It might have been an old joke, but it was new to me, I think. I was sitting on one of those benches they have for shoppers to take a break on, trying to think of what I was doing there. Lotty had asked me to pick up some light bulbs,

but at the time I couldn't remember. Johnny approached me and said, "Hello, Lute. You look like a man who's contemplating life, the universe, the greater scheme of things."

"Hello, Johnny," I said. "Good to see you. I came here to buy something, and I forget what it was. Forgetfulness runs in the family. It's the Corhern in me."

"You could do worse. Did you know that diarrhea is hereditary?" he asked with a twinkle in his eye.

"No, I didn't know that."

"Oh, yes. It runs in your jeans."

Now that I've written it down, I do recall hearing it before somewhere . . .

It really doesn't make much difference what I inherit. Crossword puzzles or no crossword puzzles, if I were to inherit Uncle Tim's money, I'd just grow old and probably forget about it, anyway.

"Remember that time we travelled around the world on your Uncle Tim's money, Lute?" Nean might ask.

"Money? Uncle Tim? World? What world?"

Luther Corhern

Call of the Quill

About thirty years ago, a friend of mine, Paul Layton, went to Toronto, got himself a job in a toilet paper factory, found a girl, got married, bought a house in Richmond Hill, had two children (a boy and a girl), and settled down. Paul, being the ambitious type, worked his way up in the factory from assembly line worker to foreman, then on to assistant manager. Recently he was made manager of the whole place.

He used to come home every summer and Christmas during those early years, but as he grew busier and busier with the job and the family, his visits grew more and more infrequent, and for the last five years, up until a week ago, he either couldn't find the time or didn't have the desire to come home at all.

Last week, in the middle of March, he paid me a visit.

"Paul! Come in! Come in!" I greeted him. "I haven't seen you for years! What brings you to the Miramichi at this time of year? Nothing wrong, I hope."

"No, no. Just needed a break."

Paul's fifty or so, a bit older than me. Twenty years ago, he was slim, had thick black hair, tanned skin, an easy smile, and a mischievous look in his eye. Last week, when he stepped into my kitchen, he could have been someone else. He was middle-aged and mostly bald, beer drinking had added a hundred or so pounds to his six-foot frame, and he obviously needed to get outdoors more — he was pale as a farmer's armpit.

I offered him a scotch, but he declined, settled for a cup of coffee. We sat at the kitchen table, and for the first fifteen or twenty minutes the conversation came with considerable effort,

small talk in its most congealed state. After a while, however, we got into it.

"You've been writing, I hear," he said.

"Oh, I started with keeping a camp log for Cavender Bill," I said almost apologetically. "You know, writing something now and again about the goings on at the Salmon Camp. Then it sort of became a hobby."

"You should be good at it, Lute. You always read a lot. Thinking about making it a profession?"

"Ha! I'm not a real writer, Paul. I just dabble."

"Well, living out here by the river, alone with nobody to bother you, you certainly have the opportunity to be a real one. Here you can think and create. A lot of people make a lot of money at it, Lute."

"Some people make a living at it. Others dabble. I'm a dabbler."

"You sound as though you might have a bit of a complex, Lute."

"Yeah, well, I'm in a rut. Sitting around here on the bank of the Miramichi River, living in a trailer, playing guitar, fly fishing for salmon, playing a little golf, perusing and musing over the works of dead poets . . . I don't know, Paul. I just don't know what's become of me."

"Men work all their lives to retire and do what you're doing!" said Paul.

"Who told you about me writing?" I asked.

"Oh, I heard about it. Nean or somebody told me."

"Well, I'm not really a writer at all."

"How do you figure that?"

"The way I see it, you're not a writer until you get rich. You can write all the books and stories you want, and if you're not rich, people will still walk up to you and ask you what you're doing for a living."

"So you keep on writing. Why? What is it with you?"

"I don't know. It's a challenge, I guess. It's stupid. I'm forever embarrassed about it. I should get a job, become a photographer or something. The only thing is that I can't seem to quit. Writing is a crutch, I lean on it. I'll probably write about this conversation after you leave. But hey, Paul, this is all about me. How's things going with you?"

"I guess compared to you I'm living in the fast lane."

"That's good."

"No, Lute, it's not good. I'm losing it. Nowadays, when I look at myself in the mirror, I see a stranger. I don't know who I am anymore. That's why I'm here, Lute. I need to find myself. I chose the middle of March to come home because it's when everything is stark and bare and natural. In March, you can step outside and smell the dog turds. Nothing's artificial, nothing's manicured. In March, you can feel the bite of winter and the caress of spring. I think I might possibly find myself out there in the hard, stained snowbanks of March.

"Remember when we were boys, Lute? Remember my grandfather and yours, and Bunny Vincent and old Fred Munn and Freeman Lewis? My grandfather would invite those old boys over, and for hours they'd do nothing but sit around and sing. Remember? You were there a couple of times."

"Yeah. Some of their songs were ten minutes long."

"They'd let us hang around as long as we didn't get in the way or make too much noise."

"So of course we rarely got to stay."

"I remember us rolling on the floor with laughter as the old men sang their crooked, funny, sometimes mournful songs. We weren't laughing at the lyrics but because hardly a one of them could carry a tune."

"Ha! Yeah, I remember."

"One evening, I was down by the river when a lonesome, mellow voice reached me from across the water, the voice of old Freeman Lewis singing 'Peelhead, He's the Boy.' I'd heard Freeman sing before, but never like he sang that night. That one song, coming to me over the river on the evening breeze, awakened in me a greater appreciation for my heritage than any other single event before or since.

"When I think of those old songs, 'The Scow on Cowden Shore,' 'The Miramichi Fire,' 'Peter Emberly,' 'The Lumberman's Alphabet,' it's like going back in time. I can smell the river, envision those old guys in long woollen underwear, open at the neck, stained at the armpits, worn all year round. I can hear the rhythm of an axe chopping into a yellow birch, taste the spruce gum, and feel the pine spills beneath my feet. Lute, I need to spend some time here, six months if I have to."

"Six months! What about your job?"

"Ah, I'm not needed. We've got telephones, computers, e-mail . . . I can run the place from here."

"So you're starting the ball rolling in March."

"You know, Lute, you're the first guy I've told about my discontent, about losing myself. Do you understand where I'm coming from?" Paul stood and went to the window, stared down on the river. "Spring. The pussy willows, April showers, the temperature creeps up, budding lilacs, the first robin, the doves on the arbour, the old Chiclet River . . ."

"Chiclet River?"

"You know what I mean. The ice floes, like Chiclets."

"Yeah, well, I guess I do, sort of."

"Three hundred and fifty years ago, a poet by the name of John Dryden summed up the writing profession in one little poem. I've been reading Dryden all my life, but it wasn't until recently that I came upon it. I liked it so much, it made so much sense, that I memorized it.

The midwife laid her hand on his thick skull,
With this prophetic blessing: be thou dull;
Drink, swear, and roar, forbear no lewd delight
Fit for thy bulk; do anything but write.

Dryden wrote that, I suspect, to keep writers humble to the grave. He knew what the profession was all about over three hundred years ago and wrote it down for all of us to see. But, damn it, I don't know, I just don't know. I'm the one who's in a rut, Lute."

"I don't think you've lost yourself at all. By the way you just waxed on, I'd say you know exactly where you came from and where you're going."

"Yes, but to be able to put it in words like you, like a writer, is one thing, experiencing it is quite another. I want to catch a salmon on a fly rod, boil it in water and vinegar, and eat it with a little chow chow on the side. I want to drift on the river at night, lying on my back in a canoe so that the only visible existence is the stars above. I want to crawl from a tent on a cool morning and witness the silent vee of the salmon making their way upstream to spawn. I want to walk on the rickety footbridge at Carroll's Crossing. I want to see the river reflected in the thoughtful, loving eyes of its people, and I want to hear the stories and the songs.

"For years after I left here, I thought that beauty was a manicured lawn and a four-lane highway. I'd come down from Toronto, with its tall buildings and bustling streets, its golf courses and fancy clothes, and laugh at the Mackinaws, the car-tire planters and culvert ends I'd find here. Now those things are the most beautiful things in the world. Did you know that in Toronto these days they're using car tires for planters?"

"Ha! Shirley Ramsey did that forty years ago."

"And lawn ornaments, too, are catching on."

"Is that a fact? In Toronto?"

"In Toronto."

"Do they have doorsteps?"

"Yes, but they'll learn."

"Ha!"

"Well, I gotta be going, Lute. Thanks for listening."

"Well, if there's ever anything I can do to help . . ."

"Just be here, Lute."

"I'm not going far, that's for sure. I'm thinking I might take a drive down to the village and hang out for a while at John's Diner. Want to join me? Maybe we can get filled in on the latest gossip."

"That sounds like fun, Lute, but I've got some things I need to do."

"What's so important that you can't join me for a couple of hours?"

"Ah, well, just a few things I need to get cleared away. But I'll meet you there tomorrow."

"Great."

"See you tomorrow, then."

"Yeah."

He was going through the door when he turned and asked, "Is there a Saint Patrick's Concert happening at the Catholic Hall this year, Lute?"

"I . . . I don't really know. I haven't seen any posters. I guess not."

"Too bad. It went on for eighty years. Well, I'll see you tomorrow. Keep on writing, Lute."

Paul wasn't any further than the end of the driveway when I went to my old typewriter and tried to put something on paper. I thought for a long time, wrote for a while, trashed it, thought some more. I thought about Paul, about being in a

rut, about what I'd said to him about not being a writer unless you get rich doing it. That was stupid. I left my typewriter and went to the same window that Paul had watched the river from, tried to see the scene through his eyes. The Chiclet River. It's funny how you can blush over something you're only remembering. I went back to the typewriter. After a couple of hours, as if the muses were trying to tell me something, I realized that I had written almost nothing at all.

The call of the quill. Who am I?

Luther Corhern

Flood Talk

We were all at Stan's Convenient Store one night in late March when Nean Kooglin straightens right up, yawns, and says, "Last fall, the moon stayed pretty much to the north, so I knew the winter was gonna be cold."

"Yeah," puts in Lindon, also yawning. "Oh, yeah, yeah, yeah. Cold winter, yeah. That's, that's, that's right, Nean old dog, cold winter, yeah."

"Jim Fraser, the butcher from Renous, said the pig's milt was longer than usual, and you lads know as well as I do that that's a sign of a long winter," continues Nean as if Lindon didn't exist. "Come to think of it, last summer the hornet nests were high off the ground, and that's a sign of deep snow."

"So, what're ya comin' at?" asks Elvis, catching the old yawning bug.

"Well, the moon, the pig, and the hornets were right on the button, for we had a long, cold, snowy winter. I think the only sunny day we had in the month of February was Groundhog Day."

"She's not like she used to be, though," says Elvis. "She used to be a lot colder when we were operatin' under Fahrenheit. Old Celsius don't seem to have the bite in it, so it don't."

"She's colder than a moose yard every winter as far as I can see," I added. "It don't take no pig's milt or hornet's nest to tell me that. It's the rest of the year that I find a bit up in the air."

"What I always wondered was, if a pig's milt here in New Brunswick was, oh, say, six inches long, how long would it be in Florida?" asked Elvis. "A half inch? An inch?"

"Prob'ly," said Nean. "And on the other hand, a pig way up in the Arctic might have a milt a yard or two long."

"Look just like a walkin' shish kebab!" said Lindon.

"Shad flies moving about on the snow can sometimes be a clue that spring's coming, but more often than not, you'll see them one day out there enjoying the sun, and the next day they're froze solid," put in Elvis.

"Well, the winter don't seem to be ready to break up yet, anyway," I said. "The snow's still deep — there must be three feet right out in the fields and even more in the woods. If it stays around too late and then warms up, we'll have a flood sure as hell."

"There's a lot of ice in the river, too," said Nean. "A flood would do a lot of damage if it come along right now."

"I ain't gonna buy my peach rubbers yet for a while," commented Lindon.

Purry Porter was there, but he didn't say a word, just grinned to himself like an old wizard. And, come to think of it, that's about all the rest of us had to say on the subject, too. We got to talking about something else and went home at about ten o'clock as we always do.

Well, about two nights later Purry Porter showed up at Stan's wearing a brand new Mackinaw and peach rubbers. A Mackinaw is a woollen coat that comes in various colours: red and black, green and black, blue and black, always checked. Peach rubbers are the ones with the yellow soles and green tops. They reach to just below the knee and have three or four eyelets at the top. When you see a Mackinaw, spring is coming, because it's not heavy enough for the cold of winter. But it also suggests that the spring will be a cold one, because a Mackinaw is too heavy for any kind of warm weather. When you see Purry Porter in peach rubbers, you can safely assume that we're in for a lot of rain.

Well, anyway, Purry showed up that night, dressed like I told you, and sure enough, the very next day a big old sou'wester came up the river with about two inches of rain on its wings and swept away about half the snow. Then the sun came out for three or four days, then it rained some more. Spring was definitely in the air, and everyone in the neighbourhood was amazed at Purry's forecasting ability.

I live pretty close to the river, and on the twelfth of April I was awakened in the middle of the night by the thunder and roar of the ice moving about, packing up for its voyage to the Atlantic. It was a dark and rainy night, which bothered me a bit because I always like to watch the ice going out. Watching it pile up and jam, let go, pile up and jam again, the water rushing, backing up and flooding, letting go and rushing — it's a wonderful thing to watch.

One year, back in the early seventies, we had a snowless winter with temperatures so low that you had to read the thermometer with a dipstick. With so little snow, the ice on the river froze three feet thick. Then, one day in February, the temperature rose and it started raining. It poured for three days. There was water everywhere! And with no snow to sponge it up, and with the ground frozen harder than Dotty Barker's molasses cookies, the water had no place to go except to the river.

The river came up fifteen or twenty feet in less than a day, and with all that heavy ice, all hell broke loose.

The Cains River ice let go first, and out toward the Miramichi it went. The trouble was that the Miramichi, being a much larger river than its tributary, was not ready to cough up its ice just yet, and the two rivers got into a bit of a scrap. Of course, the Miramichi, being the bigger river, won the battle, and the Cains River ice had no choice but to pile up.

So it piled and piled and piled, and all the time the water

kept backing up and flooding until it got to be so heavy that something had to snap. But the old Miramichi, at least below the mouth of the Cains, wouldn't give an inch. On the other hand, *above* the mouth of the Cains, the Miramichi was not so able, and that was the weak point that the Cains took advantage of.

The Cains River water, ice, everything went up the Miramichi! For a whole hour it went up the Miramichi!

For a whole hour, witnesses above the mouth of the Cains watched the Miramichi River flowing backwards!

When the ice below the mouth of the Cains finally let go, all hell broke loose again. Ice, camps, vehicles, boulders, houses, sawmills, everything went down the river. Trees as big around as garbage cans snapped and splintered as if they were toothpicks. One bridge rammed the next bridge, those two rammed the third, and so on until there wasn't a bridge left from Juniper to Bay du Vin.

I missed out on the up-river action, the river running in the wrong direction, but with my trailer just two inches above the flood level, I had quite enough excitement. I vacated, of course, when I saw what was happening, and I was more than just a little surprised and delighted when I returned the next day and found the trailer still there and undamaged. Others, not so lucky, lost everything. Some, on the other hand, actually came out of the flood richer than ever. Dougie Shaffer, for instance, built himself a new house, barn, garage, boathouse, and three sporting camps from the lumber that drifted down from the Doaktown mill and came to rest in front of his house. The only things he had to buy were nails and a few rolls of tarpaper.

Anyway, that was in the middle of the winter, and we had no omens, no signs to read. Not even Purry Porter anticipated that little bit of teasing from nature.

This year, the ice went out like a thief in the night on the

twelfth of April, and there weren't too many Miramichiers that I know who regretted it. The ice going out is a sign of spring that no one ever contests, especially us guys who like fishing and guide for a living.

On the very same day, Lindon quit tying flies, Nean closed up his boat-building shop, Elvis quit repairing nets and canoes, Purry quit making his antique lobster traps, and I quit making canoe poles. It was time to get the old rods out, lines dressed, reels greased, boats in, motors mounted. By the time the season opened for black salmon fishing on the fifteenth, we were all ready with our new Mackinaws and peach rubbers, the works. The ice going out in the night on the twelfth like that gave the river three whole days to clear and settle, so every one of us caught fish on opening day. As a matter of fact, I had six hooked, landed, and released before noon.

I was fishing at the mouth of MacKenzie Brook, a great place for black salmon, and I had just landed number six when I noticed smoke curling from the chimney of the Salmon Camp. That, I knew, could mean only one thing. Cavender Bill was back. And no more than a minute or two after I saw the smoke, I saw Nean motoring in that direction. Five minutes later, Elvis motored up the river and pulled ashore in front of the Salmon Camp.

I was a happy lad, I tell ya! There's no happier time than when, on opening day, the boys get together, have a few drinks, and swap a few yarns with Cavender Bill. Every spring when Cav lands from Texas, he has a new Cadillac, new stories to tell, and a jug or two of duty-free liquor. I didn't waste any time joining the group, and I had just stepped into the camp when Purry and Lindon showed up.

"The gang's all here!" said Cavender with that big grin of his, and we all knew that he was in good shape and genuinely glad to be back.

He poured us all a drink and, always being more than generous, was about to pour us a second round when Nean reminded everybody that we should consider going fishing for a while first and do the drinking later. Everyone agreed with that little suggestion. We all knew very well that the river in April was no place to be with a belly full of liquor.

We all wanted to go fishing, but we also wanted to be together, to have a say and a few laughs. So, instead of going out and anchoring our boats here and there all over the place, we motored down to the old McDougall farm, pulled up, built a fire, and fished from the shore, casting out as far as we could. We were like a bunch of kids playing hooky with no chance of getting caught. We took turns fishing, gathering wood, and tending the fire, and we caught and released so many salmon that we didn't even bother to count. At one point, Lindon Tucker hooked into one that we figured would tip the scales at more than twenty pounds. That same fish, we guessed, would have weighed more than thirty pounds when it first entered the river in September last year.

When we had our fill of fishing, we headed back to the camp where we drank, ranted, raved, argued, and laughed away the rest of the day. When suppertime rolled around, we went outside, baked a bunch of potatoes, and barbecued a couple of grilse over hardwood coals in the cool April twilight.

After eating, we got down to some serious drinking, toasting the salmon, the river, and each other a good many times, forgetting, I suppose, that we had made the same toast a few minutes before. I know I got pretty loaded because I sang that old song that goes:

> *I grow my potatoes, I got twenty-five bags,*
> *I got my eight salmon and I'll get me eight more,*
> *'Cause I'm boilin' my tags.*

I had to be fairly drunk to sing that.

And along about midnight, Cavender Bill turned to Purry and asked, "Hells bells, Perry" — Cav always calls Purry Perry for some reason — "how come you're making antique lobster traps?"

"Because it's a profitable business," said Purry. "I build them out of old weathered laths and sell them to people from the west, Ontario, places like that."

"Why the hell would anyone buy an old, weathered lobster trap?"

"Can't say for sure, but I sell a good many of them every year, and them people from out west take them back with them and put them in their parlours and call them antiques. You know, around here a car from Ontario with a lobster trap on top is one of the first signs of summer."

Well, we all perked right up and leaned right in when Purry said that, I tell you, Purry the weather wizard letting us in on one of his secrets.

It was Elvis Glasby who was curious enough to ask the question in all our minds. "Tell me, Purry. How is it you know when spring is comin'?"

"Elvis, my friend, I'll tell ya," said Purry. "Spring always seems to come right after all you lads start talkin' about the possibility of a flood. When I hear you guys talkin' flood, I head right out and buy my Mackinaw and peach rubbers. And you know, for some unknown reason, it works every time."

* Log *

April 15

Caught over 20 black salmon and grilse within a mile of the Salmon Camp. As usual this time of year, Smelts and Micky Finns are the most productive flies.

Luther Corbern

The Virtual Time Machine

The other night, Kid Lauder dropped in to kill some time with the guys down at Stan's Convenient Store. Kid's a great storyteller, primarily because he's travelled so much and has done so many things. He'll go to any lengths for a laugh, and you never quite know where he's coming from. Sort of sucks you in, if you know what I mean.

Two weeks ago, for instance, he told us about the time he was eating in a restaurant in Epidaurus, Greece.

"It was getting late," he told us. "And the owner of the restaurant was starting to close the place for the night. Lil and me were the only ones left. During dinner, we had downed about six bottles of this stuff called retsina. Tastes like it was aged in a tin can, kind of a pine or turpentine taste to it."

"Don't sound like a very good drink," commented Nean.

"Well, it's not very good, but it's got a pretty good kick to it, and Lil and me were flying pretty high, chatting up a storm and all of that. Then this lad walks through the restaurant with the skinned carcasses of two sheep flung over his shoulder. And then, right behind him, another lad walks through with two more sheep. And behind him comes another and another and another, and then the first lad goes through once again, and so on, all carrying sheep carcasses. They did that for the longest time."

"So, how many sheep did they carry in?" asked Stan from behind the counter.

"Well, I don't rightly know," says Kid. "We fell asleep."

We all laughed, look here, until the tears ran down our cheeks.

Now, the other night when he showed up, he started right in talking about computers, said Lil owned one for years and had just recently got onto the Net.

None of us lads knows much about computers, but because it was a new and different sort of thing to talk about, we gave Kid room.

"You can write a letter and send it off to Europe or Japan in a matter of a few seconds," Kid told us. "The best outfit you ever seen, if you know how to use it."

"And Lil can do that?" I asked.

"Yes, sir. She's a regular whiz at it. You should have one, Lute, you doing so much writing and all. You need a computer."

"Well, I don't know, Kid. Sounds kind of high tech to me. How about you? Can you use it?"

"Well, no, I'm not that swift at it yet, but I'm learning something new every day."

"You have to stay at 'er and learn, is what I always say," commented Stan. "You're never too old to learn."

"A couple of days ago, I was playing around with it and discovered something I'm betting very few people know," said Kid. "At first, I found it hard to swallow, myself."

"Oh, yeah? What's that?" asked Shad Nash.

"Well, I'll tell you all about it. As a matter of fact, boys, I have something right here in my pocket I want you to take a look at. What do ya think of that?"

Kid took a piece of paper from his pocket and passed it around for us to read. We saw a bunch of numbers and letters and dots and things, and underneath was a short note.

Dear Kid,
A salmon and three grilse on the 25th of September.
Yours always,
Kid

None of us knew quite what to think and handed him back the letter.

"That's the proof," said Kid.

"Proof of what?" I asked.

"Well, before I told you this story, I wanted to prove to you that I'm telling the truth. You see, the other day when I was fooling around on the computer, I decided to write myself a letter and date it a year in the future. That would be, like, April fifteenth, 1999. I was figuring I'd get the letter sometime after that date next year, at which point I'd write myself back. I figured that the computer, being a machine that only does what it's told to do, would be able to handle the experiment with no trouble at all, and that it would indeed hold onto the letter until the proper time and date came along for it to be sent."

"And?"

"Well, sir, I underestimated the darn computer."

"How's that?"

"Well, it not only sent the letter to myself a year in the future, but my future self answered me and sent the answer back. Here it is right here. When I wrote myself, I simply asked, 'How was the fishing?' And this is the reply I got."

"Well, well, well," said Stan. "Ain't that amazing!"

"The best thing about it is that I won't be wasting all that time beating the water. I won't have to wet a line until September twenty-fifth."

"Well, who'd have thought?"

"Yesterday, I wrote myself letters for the next hundred years. Figured I might as well get the lowdown on the whole thing."

"And?"

"Well, I'm not much of a letter writer, you understand, and I guess I never got around to writing everything, but I got this much back already. It's from me in the year 2098."

Here, he takes out this other, longer letter and begins reading to us:

Dear Kid,

Just a few lines to let you know that I'm doing the very best and that you can start looking forward to spending some intimate time with a young, future-like lady in about ninety-eight years. I'll write you more on that occurrence some other time, but right now I'll just try and answer a few of the many questions you've been sending me across the years on your ever-so-primitive e-mail system.

To start with, the province of New Brunswick, including the Restigouche and the Miramichi rivers, is now owned by a family from Bern, Switzerland. There are salmon in the rivers, but it costs more to fish for them on a single day than an ordinary person can save in a lifetime. There are two open-water pools where ordinary people are allowed to fish for chub. Nobody bothers to chub fish anymore, however. Even though our Swiss leaders introduced a catch-and-release program in 2056, too many people caught too many chubs, and, well, you can fish for a whole week and not even see a chub that's worth throwing a hook over.

Miniature golf is the number one sport in New Brunswick these days. Our Swiss leaders allowed Disney to set up a miniature golf course in every little town. It was great for the economy (all the local people now work for Disney), and New Brunswickers boast about being the best miniature golfers in the world. Bill Androv from Longmeadow won the Disney Cup last year and was presented with the keys to a 2097 Mercedes ATV for putting a hole in one on the fifth hole at the Bliss City Miniature Golf and Country Club. Bill gave the ATV to his son, Tommy, who drives it several hours every day, around and around the Androv house. His best lap so far has been 11.52 seconds. He did that after a considerable dry spell when the trench he has worn had a chance to dry up a bit.

Bill hoped the ATV would give Tommy some incentive to follow in his father's footsteps and become another great miniature golfer. Tommy, who suffers severely from agoraphobia, still refuses to remove his helmet and pick up the family putter. A great disappointment to Bill.

Ruby Spitfire's Tackle Shop is the only other business in New Brunswick other than Disney's miniature golf industry that is not owned completely by the Swiss family. It's located in the heart of Doaktown, one of the province's largest cities. Ruby sells everything to the Swiss people at cost with the stipulation that if anything breaks, she gets to fix it. Ruby is thought to be the best rod-wrapper and guide-gluer the province has ever known. She has a sign behind the counter that reads, "Let Me Be Your Second Hand."

To answer your political questions, you might be interested to know that we've imported a premier. A Conservative. Took over about a year and a half ago. Mildred Bluelips is her/his name and he/she is a transvestite from Vancouver. His/her goal is to finish the Trans-Canada Highway from Jemseg to Sussex.

You might also be interested to know that Stan's Convenient Store went out of business about a hundred years ago, when he refused to treat the boys with the pint of rum he kept under the counter. The boys just stopped showing up and left him so very much alone.

Well, myself, it's getting late, and that young lady is in need of my attention. I'll get back to you and fill you in on more future developments later.

Don't do anything I wouldn't do.

Your future self,
Kid

"Well, boys, what do you think of that?" asked Kid.

Nean, Shad and I were all grinning from ear to ear, thought it was the best thing we'd heard all winter. But Stan seemed puzzled, stood behind the counter scratching his chin.

"What's the matter, Stan?" asked Kid. "Didn't you like it?"

"Yeah, I liked it, but . . ."

"What's the matter, Stan?"

"Well, I just can't figure out how you can be alive and able to entertain a young lady a hundred years from now."

"Advanced medicine, of course," said Kid.

"Well, does that mean that I . . ."

"No, Stan, I've been meaning to tell ya . . . you . . ."

"Never mind! Hows about a little drink, boys?"

Luther Corbern

A Rainy Day Friend

Thinking back on it, I guess I had a tough winter. I'm not a winter person. Sometimes I wish I were a fly, freeze when it gets cold and awaken when it gets warm. The life span of a fly is only twelve days, but all twelve days are fair.

I shouldn't complain, I suppose. I got the winter in, spring is here, the birds are back. I'm guiding again, I survived.

The first man I guided this year was a guy from Pennsylvania, a truck driver by the name of Thomas.

Thomas only stayed for two days, but we had a great time.

He came with two friends, Wally and Jeff. Nean guided Wally and Elvis guided Jeff.

It's funny how things work out. Nean went and picked them up at the airport, and immediately, just as soon as they got out of the car at the Salmon Camp, I knew Thomas would be my client, my sport. Maybe it has something to do with my preference for guiding good fishermen and the adventurous type. I like hearing them talk about the exotic places they've visited, the big fish they've caught, the strange foods they've eaten. I knew right away Thomas was that type of guy. He was a man of stature, had a far-off look in his eye. When we shook hands, he called me Lute, just like my friends do.

I assembled his rod, bailed the boat, started up the old outboard, and we were off down the river under a grey sky in a drizzling rain. Conditions were perfect, the salmon plentiful, expectations high.

I pulled in, killed the motor, and dropped the anchor at the mouth of Little Brook. A couple of beavers were swimming about where the river backed into the brook's small estuary, a woodpecker hammered on a nearby birch, a couple of ravens chatted in the alders.

"It's good to be back," I said.

"Back? You were on a trip?" he asked.

"No. It's good to be back to the river, to the springtime."

"Well, it's good to be here."

That was how the conversation started.

Sometimes you can sit in a boat all day with a sport and the only conversation that transpires is about fishing. The sport is often a big city guy and might as well be an alien from outer space, if you're a river boy like me. But Thomas was different. He knew how to fish, had caught more big salmon and trout in his day than old Ted Williams. He could cast ninety feet of line and present a fly as if it were on the wing. He was also aware of what fly fishing is really all about, that it's not just about catching fish, that it's about being on a beautiful river, observing nature. That it's about relaxation and camaraderie.

I've guided people who came all the way from Boston or New York or Chicago who were so stressed with the pace of big city life that they could hardly sit still for a moment. They came up here to relax and get away from it all, but instead they added to their stress by the need to catch fish. Every good salmon fisherman knows that if you go to the river with the thought that you're going to catch a salmon, you're going to be disappointed. Just being there is what it's all about. Catching a salmon has to be considered a bonus.

Like many Americans, Thomas was a loud talker. I think the guys up around the bend and downstream could hear him speaking as plain as I could there in the boat four feet away from him. A couple of times, thinking that perhaps he might be disturbing the ambiance for others, I was tempted to ask him to lower his voice, but I thought, what the hell, if they don't want to hear us talking, they can move. It's a big river.

Sometimes he seemed to be bragging a bit, but it never seemed to be coming from usual sources like conceit, competitiveness, an inferiority complex. No, his bragging, if you could call it bragging, came from his heart, from his pride in his wife, his children, the success of his friends and neighbours.

We talked about politics, trucking, and serial killers. We talked about the cost of living in the United States compared to Canada. He talked about his German shepherd dog, gardening, reading, writing, and sports. We talked about more personal things, like family. He told me about his daughter, who had a rare disease. He told me about his wife, whom he loved and felt lucky to have, about the shrine she built to the Virgin Mary and how she was at home at that very moment putting the finishing touches on it by shovelling tons of gravel. He told me about his son's prowess on the soccer field and his younger daughter, who was the apple of his eye. He told me about how once, when he was a kid, his father punished him for drinking, and he had to take it even though he had not been drinking. "I'd really been smoking dope, and I wasn't about to tell my father that."

Sometimes when you're guiding some fellow who's looking down his nose at you and your occupation, at the trailer you live in and the old vehicle you drive, the days can seem extremely long. To Thomas I was an equal, and the days went quickly. We talked, we fished, we smoked, we were happy to be there, we even enjoyed the rain. On the second day, during the last hour before we were to head back to the Salmon Camp and bid our farewells, a sense of melancholy fell upon us. We were becoming friends, and the realization that he would soon leave and we'd probably never see each other again had drifted into the scene.

"I have at least five years of hard work ahead of me," he said. "I don't get fishing much. But I think I'll start fishing with my son."

"That's a good idea," I said.

There's a stream near where I live."

"Yeah?"

"If you're ever down Pennsylvania way . . ."

"I don't travel much. Maybe, someday."

"Hey! The sun's trying to come through."

"Yeah. It's supposed to clear."

"You know, Lute, it's been drizzling and we haven't caught any fish, but these have been two of the best days I've had in a long time."

"Yeah, it's always good to get out on the water."

"I think we should keep in touch. I'll leave you my address and phone number."

"Sure. Sounds good. I see the other guys have gone back to the camp. I suppose we should . . ."

"Just a few more minutes," he said. And then, for the first time in the two days, he stopped talking. He just sat there and looked at the river. He seemed to be feeding on it, digesting it — the grey sky, the budding alders, the wildlife.

"I'm sorry you didn't catch any fish," I said. "With this rain, I guess the water was a bit cloudy."

"But the sun will rise tomorrow," he said. "Let's go."

I pulled the anchor and started the motor. Back at the camp, we exchanged addresses and phone numbers, and he and his friends were off.

Cavender Bill and I watched them drive away.

"Can you guide again tomorrow?" asked Cav.

"I . . . I don't know."

"I'm expecting the Gutman party in any minute. You'll be guiding John Bernstein, owner of John's Surplus in Boston."

"I don't know."

"What's the matter, Lute? You look like you lost your best friend."

"Ah, nothin'. I'm just a little melancholy. It goes with the turf, I guess."

"What d'ya mean by that?"

"It's called the hospitality business. All us guys are paid to be hospitable. Most of the people that come here to fish need a guide about as much as they need two rear ends. It seems most of these people come here and pay us to fish with them, except it's illegal for a guide to fish while he's guiding, so they're really paying us to be their friends. It should be called the friendship business. These people are buying friendship."

"Friends that you have to buy are seldom worth what you pay for them, Lute. That guy you were guiding . . .'

"Thomas."

"Yeah, Thomas. Thomas didn't buy your friendship, Lute, you gave it to him. You know how it's done, Lute. You have a knack for it. You know that the only way to have a friend is to be one. Cheer up. You've done a good thing, you've made a friend. Fuller said: Make not a bosom friend of a melancholy soul."

"Hmm."

"Now, can you guide in the morning?"

"Yeah, I suppose. This one will be a fair weather friend, I guess."

"What's that?"

"Oh, nothing."

* Log *

April 30

9:45 A.M. One salmon. 8 pounds. Caught by Elvis Glasby's sport, Jeff Maxwell.

11:00 A.M. Lindon Tucker's sport, Henry Davidson, lost a huge salmon, swears it was too bright and aggressive to be a black.

2:15 P.M. Nean Kooglin's sport, Wally Jacobson, landed a small grilse.

2:45 P.M. Cavender Bill landed a 12-pound salmon.

Fishing is slowing down. The blacks have about moved out and the brights aren't in.

Luther Corhern

Holidays

Cavender Bill is gaining a reputation as one of the better out-fitters on the Miramichi River. Every year he finds himself booking on more and more guests.

This spring, when he drove in from Texas and opened up the Salmon Camp for the season, the first thing he told me was that he intended to build another camp.

"Right now, Lute, I can only comfortably accommodate eight people a day. I could book on twice that many if I had more room. I'm putting up a new camp right there beside the main camp. We need two more bedrooms, a bathroom, and a dining room."

"Building another camp and having more people in is one thing," I said. "But it'll mean you'll need more water, another pool."

"I've looked after that," he said. "I've leased the Twin Channel Pool. If all goes well, I have first option to buy it. Hell, I like that pool so much I might buy it anyway."

This was the best news I'd heard in a long time. The Twin Channel Pool gets its name from the fact that it's located where the channel splits evenly and runs fast and deep around both sides of a little island. The upper end is good in high water and the lower end produces well in low water. It's one of the best pools on this section of the river.

Cav was true to his word. He's got all kinds of money and is the kind of a lad that can make things happen. Within a few days, a crew of masons, carpenters, and labourers were on the site, and it was amazing how quickly that building went up. Within three weeks, painters, plumbers, and electricians were called in, and a few days after that, the furniture arrived. One month from the day he first mentioned it to me, the camp was finished, the grounds were cleaned up, and everything was ready for the first party of sports to move in.

It takes a lot of careful organizing to get a job like that done so quickly and efficiently, and you have to hand it to Cavender Bill. He's the best darn organizer I've ever seen. He has a way of getting more out of a man than can be expected, but he does it in such a way that nobody ever complains. He had Nean Kooglin and me going from morning to night, seven days of the week, for example, and I think if Cav had wanted more from us, we would have given it to him.

Anyway, when the job was complete, Cav called us into his office, gave us a cigar, and poured us a drink.

"I want to thank you fellas," he said. "Without you two, the job would not have moved along so quickly. We're a week ahead of schedule."

We toasted Cav and he toasted us, and it was plain to see that all three of us felt pretty good about the whole thing.

"I'm taking off for a week," said Cav. "I'm flying to Arizona. My daughter's there, and I'd like to spend some time with her."

"That's the very best," said Nean. "You take off and have a good time. Me and Lute kin look after things here."

"Well, Nean, I've been thinking. There's really nothing to look after. We're a week ahead of schedule, and I haven't anybody booked on until the twentieth of the month. Now, you two have worked so hard and have been so good about everything that, well, I think maybe you deserve a little bonus. I want you both to take a vacation. A real vacation."

"A vacation?" I asked.

Other than the occasional spree in Saint John, neither Nean nor myself had ever taken a vacation in our lives.

"Now, don't get me wrong," said Cavender Bill. "It won't

cost you a cent. You decide where you want to go and I'll pay for the trip. Nothing elaborate, mind you, but I wouldn't mind sending you both to Montreal or Boston for a few days to give you a taste of the big city. Hows about it, boys? Feel like introducing yourselves to the rough and tumble of the big city? Where would you like to go?"

"Ah, I don't know," said Nean. "Never been very far. Never really thought about it."

"Well, think about it, boys. Let me know by tonight or tomorrow morning and I'll arrange it."

"Thanks a lot, Cavender Bill, but . . ." I tried.

"No buts! Just let me know and I'll look after everything. I have to know right away, though, because I'm flying out of here tomorrow night."

Nean and I left Cavender in his office and went up to my old trailer to do some serious thinking. A vacation was something we had never thought about before.

"You know what I've always wanted to do?" said Nean. "I've always wanted to fish for them big steelhead trout ya read about in the magazines."

"Me, too," I said. "But those things are in the rivers out west, aren't they? I mean, I don't think he's talking about sending us halfway round the world."

"Yeah, I guess you're right. Too costly. So where would you like to go, Lute?"

"Well, Cav mentioned Montreal and Boston. Maybe that's where we should go. Montreal for a few days."

"What for?"

"Ah, I . . . I . . . to see the big city."

"I hear there's pretty good trout fishing in Maine. Maine's not too far away. He'd prob'ly send us to Maine."

"I could save him a pile of money and go fishing trout right back here on the North Lake."

"That's true. And you know, it kind of looks like we might get a run of salmon. I hear they're picking up a few in Quarryville."

"Yeah, I heard that, too. And now that we have the Twin Channel Pool to fish in — so, how about Boston? Ever been to Boston?"

"No. Maybe Boston. What do ya do in Boston, Lute?"

"Well, you take buses, stay in hotels and drink . . . ride elevators . . . I'm not quite sure, Nean."

"We gotta think of something. Good old Cav's given us a chance in a lifetime to see the world. I say we go fishin' in Maine. They get them big brown trout down there, and pickerel . . ."

"Maybe you're right, Nean. But it would be a good racket if we went way down there fishin' trout, then come home to learn that we missed out on a big run of salmon."

We tossed one idea after another back and forth and finally came up with a plan that we thought Cav would go for. Then, back to his office we went.

"So, what have you decided?" he asked.

"Well, we sort of decided not to go very far," said Nean.

"We sort of decided to maybe take a drive into Blackville, buy some beer, and, if you don't mind, we thought maybe we'd stay right here in the new camp and fish the Twin Channel Pool."

"That's not a vacation for you fellows," said Cav. "You spend your whole lives here. Why don't you take a little trip?"

"See, we heard they're picking up a few salmon in Quarryville, and that means there might be a run coming. And you know yourself that a run can sometimes come and go in a few days. Wouldn't want to miss it," I explained.

"Yes, but . . ."

"And that's not all," put in Nean. "We want Lindon Tucker for a guide and Lotty to do the cookin'."

"Hmm. I see. Okay, if you're sure that's what you want."

"Can't imagine a better holiday," said Nean.

"If you don't mind, we'll move in tomorrow night," I said.

"Okay, boys, you got it. I'll call Betty and Lindon and set it up. But I don't want you buying the beer. I'll stock the bar."

"The very best," I said. "But there's just one more little thing. If ya don't mind, if it's all right with you, could you not tell Lindon who he'll be guidin'?"

Cavender thought for a moment, then grinned. "What time do you want him to show up?"

"Well, Lindon don't usually go out until about eight. I'd say, maybe, would six o'clock be all right with you, Nean?"

"Hell! That's a bit late. I'd say five."

"All right," said Cav, still grinning. "Five o'clock. Have fun, boys."

Cav left for Arizona the next night, and Nean and I moved in. We put on our very best fishing clothes and hats and stepped around in that beautiful new camp with drinks in our hands and big cigars lit up, just like we were millionaires from the States. Lotty cooked us up a big fancy dinner that we washed down with some high-priced red wine, then we sat on the veranda to watch the river and chat about just how lucky we were.

The river was peaceful and calm, parr were jumping, the birds were singing, and about every five minutes a school of salmon coursed its way up through the pool. I played the guitar and we took turns singing some good old Hank Williams songs, the sun went down and reddened up the horizon for about an hour, then the stars came out. It was like being in Heaven.

Lindon Tucker hates getting up early, and when he showed up at five o'clock the next morning, he was grumpier than a wet tomcat.

When he stepped into the camp to see us lads, he said, "Where's the crazy hoot owls that wants to go fishin' in the middle of the night?"

"We're the crazy hoot owls," said Nean. "And it's five after five. You're late!"

"You mean, I came all the way down here and there ain't no sports?"

"Y'all are lookin' at the sports," I said in my best American accent. "Me, Luther Corhern, and Mr. Nean Kooglin here are your bigshot champion fly-casters for the rest of the week. We'll be fishin' the Twin Channel Pool. Now, do y'all have any advice on what flah we might tie on our fancy and expensive gear?"

"You mean, I came all the way down here to . . ."

"That's right, Linny, me boy," said Nean, pulling on his waders. Nean's waders must be ten or fifteen years old and have been patched so many times that they look like a Scrabble board. Nean's feet are about three sizes bigger than Lindon's, and he's about a foot taller.

"Now, Linny, me boy," continued Nean, "if Mr. Corhern here and myself have a good week and hook into some good big salmon, I'll be very, very grateful and see that you're well rewarded. How'd you like to have these waders, Linny?"

"Those things?"

"That's right, Linny, me boy. Show me and Mr. Corhern here a good time and they're yours."

Looking at the patches upon patches on those old green rubber waders of Nean's, even Lindon had to break down and laugh.

That morning was the beginning of the best week of fishing and good fun, the best holiday I ever had. Lindon joined in on the fun and played the part of the guide just as we played the parts of the sports for the rest of the week. He netted our fish, carried our gear, tied our hooks on, changed our leaders . . . at times I think he was a better sport than either one of us. At the end of the week, I told him honestly that he was the best guide

I'd ever had. When Cav landed back from Arizona, I told him that he was the best outfitter I'd ever had, and I was being honest there, too.

And you know, being the sportsman gave me a whole new perspective on what it's like to experience the Miramichi River. You see the river, the fields, the forest, and the sky in a different way; you see this as a place that any normal person on any kind of a regular schedule has too little time for. You probably think it's funny that a Miramichi guide would spend his vacation fishing the very same river he fishes every day, but if I could afford it, I'd do the same thing next year. As Cavender Bill would say, "Hells bells! I might even retire here."

* Log *

June 16

8:30 A.M. One salmon. 13 pounds. Caught by Lindon Tucker's sport, Luther Corhern. Caught in the Home Pool behind the Furlong Rock, on a No. 8 Black Bear Hair.

9:45 A.M. One grilse. 5 pounds. Caught by Lindon Tucker's other sport, Nean Kooglin. Caught in Home Pool behind Bellyview Rock, on a No. 8 Green Machine.

7:30 P.M. One grilse. 5 pounds. Caught by Nean Kooglin in the lower end of the Twin Channel Pool, on a No. 8 Green Machine.

8:00 P.M. One grilse. 4 Pounds. Caught by Luther Corhern in the lower end of the Twin Channel Pool, on a No. 8 Smurf.

Luther Corhern

The Tiger's Extinct at Riverbend

For me, gardening is one of the greatest, most rewarding hobbies in the world.

I'm not a great gardener, but I take great pleasure in going to work out back — turning the sod, shaking free the fertile earth and worms, levelling the beds, planting seeds in straight lines, covering and tamping them down, zippering them up with my old garden rake. Then there's the watching and waiting, seeing the first little sprigs reach from the earth to face the sun. There's so much peace, goodness, kindness, generosity, warmth, and beauty in gardening. It's God's work, I believe.

I knew a wonderful lady who entered and surveyed her garden every morning and every evening, saying things like, "There's a new cucumber plant up! The black-eyed Susans are doing well. Look, Lute, there's a couple of new things coming up in that bed over there! What do you think they are? Mmm . . . smell the lilacs!"

This ritual meant more to her, I think, than anything else she did all day.

I know how she felt out there, for I, too, enter my garden several times a day and reap the same rewards. During the winter, I see my garden in my fantasies, and it's much the same. I think about the blossoms and feel their cool, gentle caress. I'm a born dreamer, so it's not difficult for me to enjoy my garden all year round.

There are other hobbies, one of which I've been into for years.

Fishing.

It's my work, and it's my play. I love to fish and I love being on the river as much as I love entering my garden. I go to the river, wade into the water and throw sixty or eighty feet of line, watch it ess out, place the fly here and there as if it were on the wing. Sometimes I even catch a fish. There's a certain reward there. You pull in a nice, plump trout or a beautiful Atlantic salmon. And in the winter, in my dreams and fantasies, the experience is much the same. There's the lush green shoreline, the murmuring rapids, and the still pond below. The salmon, the birds, the flies, the gentle breezes, everything is there as it should be. In the spring, summer, and fall, I fish, and in the winter I play it back in my dreams. It's as easy for me to play back the memory of gardening and fishing as it is to play back the memory of that wonderful lady surveying the daily developments in her garden.

A year ago, Elvis, Nean, Purry, and I decided to get into an alternative hobby, something different, something we could do together.

"An outdoor sport," suggested Nean.

"A competitive sport," added Purry.

"There's not enough of us for a baseball team," I commented. "We're too old for that kind of running around, anyway."

We tossed around a bunch of ideas for a while, touching upon and passing by lawn bowling, hiking, jogging, tennis, badminton, swimming, horseshoes, and perhaps several more. It was Nean who finally mentioned golf.

"It's good exercise, we'll be swinging a club, be out in the fresh air, four of us can play at a time . . . what d'ya think?"

"Well, Nean, I don't know," said Elvis. "Golf could get expensive, couldn't it?"

"Well, maybe, but we don't have to go every day. Got too much guiding to do, anyway. What do ya think, Lute?"

I like watching golf on TV. Seems to be easy enough. All Norman, Faldo, Price, and the rest of those guys do is beat a little ball around with a club and put it in a little hole. It's as simple as that, and they're all multi-millionaires. "Hell," I thought, "if it does cost us some money, after a few weeks practice, we'll probably earn the money back."

"Yes," I said. "I like the idea. Let's start playing golf."

A few days later, we all climbed into Purry's van and headed for Fredericton, where we each purchased a half-dozen clubs or so and bags to put them in. We only bought one putter among the four of us. We figured since we'd all be on the green at the same time and taking turns putting, one putter would be enough.

That was the first time we went shopping.

After a few games, we realized we needed more gear. By the end of the summer, we were all decked out with as much as a thousand dollars worth of bags, balls, clubs, umbrellas, ball retrievers, tees, gloves, shoes. Nean bought an electric counter for keeping his score. Needing more distance, Elvis bought himself a big-headed driver. Purry hunted up the club pro and took half a dozen lessons, and I read everything I could get my hands on about the game. We played the course in Doaktown about three times a week, and I must say that every time out, our game improved. It wasn't long before every one of us could shoot in the seventies. One day I shot a sixty on the first nine and a sixty-two on the second nine. I'm proud of that. It was the low score of the year.

There was one thing we rarely had to buy. Balls. We were in the woods so much looking for our balls that we kept finding other people's lost balls. Spotting balls in the water hazards was nothing for lads used to spotting fish in four feet of water. I think I found about fifty. Elvis was so into finding balls that he sometimes forgot he was playing a game, and we wouldn't see him for two or three holes.

None of us ever had to yell "Fore!" We never hit a ball far enough or fast enough to hurt anybody.

One day after playing eighteen, we were having a beer in the clubhouse, and a fellow across the way asked Nean if he'd broken a hundred.

"Oh, yes," said Nean. "I think I did that back there on the thirteenth hole."

In some circles, amateur golfers allow themselves to play what they call a mulligan. It means you can hit a second ball when the first one you've driven, your tee shot, doesn't go anywhere near where you were aiming. We gave ourselves a mulligan every nine holes.

It helped our game, but not enough. So we came up with a rule of our own, one we called a donovan. Our donovan allowed us a second chance anywhere on the fairway, every hole. Toward the end of the season, we came up with the mullaly. A mullaly gave us a free putt on every green.

Perspiring in the hot sun or getting drenched in torrential rain, sometimes frustrated to the breaking point — how four supposedly sane men could enjoy such misery beats me.

But we did.

We became almost fanatical. We played, talked about it, theorized, gave each other tips until golf began to play a major role in every aspect of our lives. Even fly fishing had to stand in the shadows!

When the course closed, we cleaned up our clubs and put them away. But we still continued to talk about the sport, watch the pros on TV, and dream.

Golf dreams are the best. You visualize yourself stepping up to the tee, taking a nice easy swing, connecting perfectly with the ball, and driving it about three hundred yards straight down the middle. A little fade or perhaps a slight hook, a nice bounce, a perfect lie. Your second shot is an easy nine iron to the green, and then a one-putt for a birdie. In my dreams, I'm Tiger Woods. I'm never in trouble. Even sand traps are a piece of cake. Aim a couple of inches behind the ball, blast, and one-putt. Just like the pros, just like Tiger Woods, just like in the books.

Well, a couple of weeks ago, spring sprung and the four of us headed for Riverbend, a beautiful new golf course on the Nashwaak River. On the first hole, I selected a three iron for the tee shot. I teed up the ball, swung at it, and the reality of this cruellest of all sports began. Thunk! The three iron hit the ground about four inches behind and an inch under the ball. Stroke number one hit the side of a shed. I walked eleven yards down the fairway to my second shot. Whack! This time the ball headed for the woods, hit a tree . . . somewhere . . . I never found it. My fourth shot sliced, my fifth hooked. My approach shot went over the green and coming back I found a bunker. Then I three-putted for a nice double-triple bogey that earned me the honour for the next tee.

On the second hole, I played better, kept my head down, tightened my grip, and concentrated. I overswung, though, and three-putted for an eight. Not bad on a par four. "Getting into the game now," I thought.

On the third hole — Nean was in the water to the right, Elvis on the other side of the railway tracks to the left, Purry thirty feet down the fairway — I managed to hit a good tee shot, two hundred yards down the middle. Everyone applauded that shot. It turned out to be the only good shot of the day. In golf, when you hit a good shot, you forget all the bad ones.

On the first nine holes, I shot a seventy-three. Nean shot a sixty-eight, Purry seventy, and Elvis seventy-one. I lost five balls. Elvis found thirty-eight.

When it comes to golf, you'd be a fool to take advice from the likes of me, but I will tell you this: if you're looking for peace, harmony and relaxation; if you're needing exercise and to rid yourself of a frustration or two; if you're stressed — don't even consider golf. Go fishing, or work in the garden.

Luther Corhern

Wade Rivers

Everywhere you go these days you'll see road construction.
You'd think an election was coming. It's great, we need better
roads. New Brunswick has been the Pothole Capital of the
World for too long.

But times are changing. Not only are roads being built, but
the guys on the crews are actually working these days!

Unheard of when I was a lad.

I remember working (or not working) for the Department
of Highways back in the sixties, eight or nine of us cutting
bushes along the Dungarvon Road. To see us lolling about,
you'd think we were the laziest bunch of men who ever oc-
cupied space on this green planet.

There was a reason for our sloth-like behaviour. Money. The
longer we took to do the job, the longer we'd get paid for doing
it. To work hard and get the job done quickly would only have
shortened our period of employment. If it took you a week to cut
the bushes, you'd get paid for a week. If you took six weeks to do
it, you'd get paid for six weeks. We learned quickly how to turn a
week's work into six weeks' work. We were not all that lazy, you
understand. We just needed whatever employment we could get.
The boss understood where we were coming from and only
showed up about once a day, looked over the progress or lack of
it, then took off, never to be seen again until the next day. We'd
watch for him, and as soon as we saw him approaching in his
green Department of Highways truck, we'd all grab our axes and
chop away for however long he stayed on the site. That's all he
asked of us. Seeing us working let him off the hook, and beyond
that he didn't care. It was government money, after all.

As far as I know, there wasn't a lazy man on the crew.

I don't think laziness is in the nature of the beast, man or animal. Laziness is more of a habit, maybe even a disease. It exists somewhere in the realm of lethargy. No one is lazy. A great many are lethargic. Lethargy springs from grief, unhappiness, hopelessness, procrastination, boredom, pride, lack of encouragement and reward, perhaps a thousand things. I've never met a person who hated work, but I've met a thousand people who hated whatever job they happened to be doing. Give people something they like doing and they'll work like the proverbial beavers.

Oh, yes, I can wax on about it, but what do I know? I've never accomplished much in my life, and I suppose I should keep my mouth shut about it. Keep my mouth shut or someone will be telling me that I should be doing more. God forbid!

It was Wade Rivers, an old friend of mine, who started me thinking about laziness. Everyone knows someone like Wade Rivers. He's one of those people who makes a profession out of doing nothing. And when he does do something, he does it very slowly.

Wade Rivers lives about a mile downstream from me, and one day last week I went to visit him. You'll not mistake Wade Rivers when you see him. He's the only man I know who has a big number four Mickey Finn in his ear. About ten years ago, he hooked himself in the lobe on a windy day and never removed it. Couldn't be bothered.

I arrived to find him in the kitchen. He was seated at the table, staring at a blank page, a pen in one hand. At first I thought he was picking his nose with the other, but on closer inspection, I noticed with some relief that he was only pulling on one of the hairs sticking out of it.

"Writin' a letter, Wade?" I asked.

"Nah."

"A story?"

"Nah. Just thinking."

"What have you been up to?"

"Nothin' much. A little of this, a little of that."

"Doing any fishing?"

"No. There's no fish."

"Well, Wade my boy, I happen to know that there's a big run of salmon on. Lindon Tucker caught a salmon and a grilse last night, and Buck Hunter caught his limit both yesterday and the day before in the Firestone Pool. They told me the river's full of fish."

"That's good."

"Want to go?"

"Where?"

"Fishin'."

"Nah. I can't be bothered fishing anymore. Besides, the salmon all seem to be running up the other side of the river."

"Well, we'll fish the other side."

"I'm left handed. I hate fishin' the other side. How do you think I got this hook in my ear?"

"Oh, yeah, well . . . playing any golf these days?"

"Nah. Quit playing golf. I was becoming a fanatic at it."

"There's nothing wrong with that. Golf's good for ya, it's good exercise."

"Yeah, well, there's more important things to think about than golf. It's just a waste of time and money."

"Fishing any brook trout lately?"

"Nah. You have to be crazy to fish the brooks these days. Too many alders and the flies will eat you alive. Go back there, get all scratched up, and what for? A few little brook trout that ain't worth bringing home."

"You know what I was thinking I'd do, Wade? I was think-ing I'd take a drive up to Doaktown, visit a few of the lads up there — you know, see how the fishing is upriver. Want to go?"

"Nah. I might have to go guiding on the weekend."

It was only Wednesday.

"What are you up to these days?" he asked.

"Oh, not much. Been fishing some, playing a little golf, doing a bit of writing, guiding, ran the river from Half Moon to Burnthill a few weeks ago. Helped Cavender Bill and the boys build that new camp. Been partying a bit, took Lotty to the movies . . ."

"Partying, you say?"

"Well, not a lot. Some."

"Would you like a beer?"

"Well, sure, if you'll have one with me."

"Nah. Gave up on drinking. Quit smoking, too."

"Well, good for you. You'll live longer." And, I thought, you'll have more time to do nothing.

Wade used to be a very good guitar player.

"Playing any music these days?" I asked.

"Never picked the guitar up for six months. There's no good music anymore. The last good song was written back about 1975."

"Well, you could play the old stuff, Hank Williams, Johnny Cash, some of the old Beatle songs, Gordon Lightfoot. I used to like how you did Gordon Lightfoot."

"Can't be bothered."

Poor Wade. I feel sorry for him. He's lost interest. So much so that he didn't even have anything to talk about. I asked him if he'd been reading anything lately, and he told me he'd read *Huckleberry Finn* last year, said he reads it every August when the corn is ripe.

"Gonna read it this year?" I asked.

"Nah."

Lethargic is what he is. He needs someone to snap him out of it.

Anyway, it was that visit that got me thinking about laziness, idleness, lethargy. Wade's not lazy. I know he isn't. I've known him for a long time. He works very hard when he takes the notion to do something. He's just in a rut. I was trying to figure out what could be done for him while I was driving back from Doaktown. There was some road construction just outside the village, and I remembered an old joke of Shad Nash's. It was about a guy named Joe applying for a job, being interviewed by a high-up civil servant.

Civil servant: *What can I do for you?*
Joe: *I'm looking for a job.*
Civil servant: *What can you do?*
Joe: *Nothing.*
Civil servant: *Good, good! We won't have to break you in.*
    You're hired. Here's your coffee.

It's too bad that whoever's in charge of road builders and the like is making them work these days. Wade Rivers would have made a great one, would have been a high ranking one, when I was a lad.

But then again, he probably wouldn't bother to apply.

Luther Corhern

A Green Machine Day

I didn't get today's Salmon Camp log written until just a few minutes ago. I spent a part of the day blaming the hold-up on two things — a mosquito and the tab key on my old Remington. The problem turned out to be something quite different.

During the summer on the Miramichi, when you can't see your hand in front of you, you know that the flies are thick. When you can see your hand in front of you, that's a sign the flies are going to be thick in the very near future.

I was out on the veranda, feeling pretty good, happy as usual and working on getting my log together. I was thinking that it was going to be a pretty scarce bit of writing, considering there hadn't been a fish caught all day, and I was trying a bit harder than usual to figure out what to say. Then I thought that I'd write the truth, report that the weather was hot, that it was mid-summer, that the wind was from the east, the water was warm and low in the river, there was not enough oxygen and too much algae: the poorest ingredients for good salmon fishing. I was typing away, thinking that it was just as important to log the bad fishing as the good fishing, that we learn as much from one as the other, when Cavender Bill steps out of the camp and asks, "What's with the choink choink-a-choink choink, choink-choink?"

"What d'ya mean?" I asked.

"You know, on the typewriter. Every once in a while I hear you go choink, choink-a-choink choink, choink-choink."

"Oh, that! 'Shave and a haircut, two bits.' That's how I indent — I go, 'Shave and a haircut, two bits' on this here long bar, and it keeps the indentation the same. All I have to do is remember the rhythm. Take a look. Nice, eh?"

"Don't y'all have a tab key?" asked Cav.

"You mean this one here with 'Tab' written on it?"

"Yeah, that's the one. Why don't you use that?"

"What's it for?"

"That's how you indent. Just hit it, like this. See? There's your indentation."

"Well, well, well! For the love of the crows! Ya learn something new every day!"

Cav just shook his head as if he thought I was stupid, then started rigging his little seven-and-a-half foot Orvis, the rod he always uses when there's a run of grilse on. He was already dressed in his waders and vest. He began tying on a number eight Black Bear Hair with a red butt and yellow hackle, and he was whistling "Barney Google" under his breathe, like he always does when he thinks the fishing's good. It always amazes me how much time he puts into little things like splicing a leader or tying on a fly. You'd think, to see him frigging with the knots and clipping the loose ends just right and whistling that stupid song under his breath, that time meant nothing to him. Now, me, if I thought the fishing was good, I'd be doing that stuff while I was walking to the river. No sense wasting time, I always say.

Anyway, several minutes had passed and we hadn't spoken another word. He was whistling "Barney Google" for the second time when I decided for no reason other than to make conversation, or just maybe to move things along a bit, that I'd say something.

"Going fishing?" I asked.

He stopped his dainty little work and his whistling and just stared at me over the top of his glasses for about five seconds, maybe ten.

"Now, what's it look like I'm doing, Lute, getting ready for a rodeo?" he said finally.

"Well, I just thought . . . oh, ah . . . is there a run o' fish on?"

He didn't answer me right away. He turned, stepped off the veranda, and was about thirty feet away before he stopped, turned, and yelled back.

"Why do you always write that stupid log there on the veranda? The flies must be eating you up! Why don't you do it in the guides' camp?"

"Thanks for your concern, but I like to watch the river," I said. "I must've seen twenty, thirty schools of fish going through this morning. All grilt, I think."

"So why are you asking me if there's a run on? You already know there's a run on! And don't call them grilt! The word is grilse!"

"Sorry," I said. "It's a habit."

Cav shook his head for the third time, amazed, I think, at how stupid I was.

"See y'all later!" He strode over the hill to the river. I could hear the legs of his waders swishing and squeaking against each other as he went.

"Maybe," I mumbled.

I was in no state for writing logs at that point, I tell ya. I didn't write a word for I don't know how long. I just sat there and watched the river, feeling kind of hurt and maybe a little lonesome. It was a beautiful day — the sun shining, birds singing, a warm easterly breeze in the birches — and I wondered what was bothering Cav. I thought maybe my typing "Shave and a haircut, two bits" so many times had gotten on his nerves. Or maybe it was something worse, a business deal gone wrong back in the States, perhaps, or maybe a woman . . .

"Well," I thought, "whatever's buggin' him, there's no need of him interrupting my important work."

A mosquito landed on my arm and, without a moments hesitation, I slapped it dead. I felt a certain satisfaction in having rid the world of a worthless pest. In fact, with one slap, I had rid the world of a great many worthless pests if that dead body happened to have been a hot little female set on reproducing several thousand of her kind.

"No one ever regrets the passing of a mosquito except maybe another mosquito."

I was thinking along these lines when I heard the laughter coming from the shore. I couldn't see anybody, but I could hear the "ha, ha, has" of two, maybe three men, carried to me on the breeze. Then the laughter subsided and there were only the birds singing and the river flowing peacefully by. I could have taken it for the laughter of ghosts if I had not recognized one of the voices as Cavender Bill's.

"He's telling someone about me," I thought. "About how stupid I am. They're laughing at me."

A school of salmon silently coursed its way up the river. The only evidence, the only indication that they existed at all was the tiny vee moving as steadily, as unhindered as the passing of time. First they were coming, then they were here, and then they were gone, like laughter on the breeze.

Wild animals are like that.

I once saw a deer at the edge of a field and tried to get close to it. I sneaked up on it, came to within forty or fifty feet of it. It was grazing, then all of a sudden it picked up my scent, lifted its head, looked at me, and dashed into the woods with leaps and bounds. Gone! Never to be seen again. Like a ghost . . . like a moment in time . . . like the life of my squashed mosquito . . . like that lonesome moment when Cavender Bill disappeared over the hill, followed only by the swishing sound of his waders and later his ghost-like laughter, then silence and loneliness.

The good feeling I'd had earlier while working on the log had vanished like that, too. A few words from an irritated Cavender Bill and presto! I was hurt and lonesome and feeling stupid.

People do that sort of thing to each other a lot. Sometimes they don't even know they're doing it. I know for a fact that Cavender Bill didn't step out of the camp to greet me with the intention of interrupting me, of ruining my day. It just happened. Maybe it wasn't his fault at all. Maybe it was me. I mean, I was the one who asked the stupid questions. I was the one who'd been typing for over a year and never took the time to investigate the tab key!

So I sat there battling flies and watching the river for what must have been an hour, trying to figure out who was right and who was wrong, or if we were both to blame, and finally my mood changed.

One of the things that had disturbed me the most was how Cavender took so long tying on that number eight Black Bear Hair with the red butt and the yellow hackle. Why did that bother me so much? Why should I care if it takes him all day to tie on a fly?

And then it all came to me and I knew beyond a doubt why I had been so bothered. And, yes, my unpleasant encounter with good old Cavender had been all my fault.

You see, it had not been the tying on of the fly that had hit me as a waste of time. It was that little Black Bear Hair with the red butt and the yellow hackle.

And Cav was right! I *was* stupid. But so was he! And our spat had been sort of subliminal, all happening right there in our very smart subconscious minds.

It all adds up to this: you don't fish a Black Bear Hair with a red butt and a yellow hackle on a day like this. There was a run of grilse on, the sun was shining, the calm river was reflecting the grassy banks and forested hills, there was green algae all over the place.

Five minutes after this thought occurred to me, I found myself standing on the gravel beach behind where Cavender

Bill was fishing. He was wading in knee-deep water, about thirty feet out. Elvis Glasby and Nean Kooglin were fishing just upstream from him. It had been Elvis and Nean who had shared the joke that had conjured up the laughter I'd heard.

I called out to Elvis. "What've ya got on?"

"Butterfly! Ain't hooked a fish all day!"

"How about you, Nean?"

"Cosseboom! Rolled one an hour ago, and that's about it!"

I started wading out to where Cav was thoughtfully fishing, casting his line as expertly as any of us guys born and raised with a rod in our hands right here on the river. When he heard me approaching, he turned to watch me, his eyes as blue as the sky.

I stopped some ten feet from him and sighed. I didn't know exactly how to go about telling him what I needed to say. If I had only thought of it earlier and told him, it would have been so much easier. I don't think he knew what to expect, thought perhaps I was coming to tell him that I was quitting my job or something. All I know was that he looked sad.

"Cav?"

"Yeah?"

"It's a Green Machine day," I said, so softly only he could hear me.

He looked at me thoughtfully for a moment, then smiled the slightest bit. Then he winked, snipped off that little Black Bear Hair with the red butt and the yellow hackle, and tied on a Green Machine. When he finally turned back to his fishing, the day was the very best again.

* Log *

June 30

4:15 P.M. One grilse. 4 pounds. Caught by Cavender Bill. Caught in the Home Pool behind the Furlong Rock on a No. 8 Green Machine.

5:05 **P.M.** One grilse. 4 pounds. Caught by Cavender Bill. Caught in the Home Pool behind Aunt Sally's Rock on a No. 8 Green Machine.

We had no sports in today, and other than Cav, the only fishermen were Elvis and Nean, neither of whom landed any fish.

Luther Corhern

Walking

When I was a young man, I used to do a lot of walking. Several times a week I'd walk the four miles down the Hemlock Road to the village, walk up and down through the village several times from canteen to dance hall to friends' houses and so on, then walk home again. One night Peter Lutz and I walked to the village and back, decided we'd like to have some wine, so walked to the village and back a second time. Not including the miles we put in on socializing in the village, we walked sixteen miles that night.

Walking was a way of life, was included in just about every aspect of existence. You walked to parties or to meet a friend; you walked to see a lover and you walked with your lover; you walked to work and back again; you walked to be with somebody and you walked to be alone.

And you were allowed to walk back then. People expected to see you walking. Nobody cared where you went. If you came to a fence, you simply climbed over it. Fences and gates were things to keep a cow in its rightful pasture and that was all.

"Who's that crossing the field?"

"Oh, that's Lute, on his way to Stan's."

"And there goes Fred Holt up the lane to Dooper's. Must be cake day."

Fred Holt was the fastest walker I've ever known. Most people had to run to keep up with him. You'd see him going with a burlap bag roped to his back and you'd know he was going to Dooper's Store for his weekly supply of cake. At Dooper's, he'd buy every cake, cookie, tart, and pie in the store, pack it all in the bag, and walk home again so fast you'd

124

think somebody's life depended on his speedy return, that the cake in his bag was an essential ingredient in his family's diet, that they'd starve to death if he didn't get it to them immediately.

Sometimes I think there are fewer paths these days, but it's probably more accurate to say that the paths are still there, there's just more barriers. Walk across somebody's field nowdays and you'll get yelled at sure as hell. You're expected to follow a fixed path and that's it. Last week in Fredericton, I noticed a fence around a cemetery. I wondered if it was there to keep the living from going in or the dead from coming out.

Today we drive everywhere, we're on line to explore the web, let our fingers do the walking. No wonder golf is so popular; we're allowed to walk on the grass, we can go where the little ball bounces. The rivers, even the forests have certainly lost their quietude.

I don't know, I'm not a scholar, I don't know much about anything. But it seems to me that walking is a good thing. To step outside and walk a mile or two across fields and over little bridges, follow streams, enter valleys, and climb hills at a pace that allows you to stop and see things, to smell the flowers and breathe the air — it has to be good for the soul, the constitution, the body, everything.

Nobody walks anymore. I know a guy who drives his pickup over the hill to the river to fish, steps into his canoe, starts up his five-horsepower outboard motor, and heads for the hot spot a mere hundred yards away.

The other day, I was weeding my garden when Ken Hunter dropped by. Ken is a poor man, lives in a small house on a piece of cleared land no bigger than a regular city lot. His house and garden take up more than half of his space, which leaves him with a lawn not a lot bigger than a postage stamp, the vegetation consisting mostly of plantain and dandelions. And guess what he bought? A sit-on lawn mower. He drove it the two hundred yards down to visit me the other day.

Over the roar of the engine, he shouted, "How do ya like my new lawn mower?"

"Great machine," I said, hoping I was showing a bit of enthusiasm.

"I've been wantin' one for a long time," he said. "Fifteen hundred dollars! With the shed I had to build to put it in, I spent over four thousand dollars. Saved up for it, I did. Took me three years."

"With a machine like that, you could mow both our lawns." My own lawn needed mowing, and I thought perhaps he was going to be neighbourly and mow my grass for me.

"Yep. Sure could. I could mow half the lawns on the Hemlock Road if I had a mind to. If I had a mind to, I could pay for this baby by mowing lawns, but that kind of activity would only wear it out, don't ya think?"

"Yeah, probably would."

And then, without another word, he drove off. In the forty-some years I've known him, I've never known Ken Hunter to say hello or goodbye.

A couple of months ago, three friends and myself ran the Miramichi River from Half Moon down to Burnthill. It's scenic and exciting, a wonderful section of the river to run. And one of the best things about that upriver stretch was that there were no vehicles anywhere, no outboard motors, no ATVs, no four-wheel drives.

One evening, we were camping at a little place with a view on a bend, and we saw an older man poling his canoe upstream toward us. The man was so quiet and peaceful, so serene; he seemed as much a part of the river as the birds and the fish.

That man poled his own canoe and walked to the river to get to it.

Walking and poling . . . rare things these days.

* Log *

July 9

The water is too warm and shallow for good fishing. The salmon are moving into the brooks. Yesterday I saw a lad landing a salmon at the mouth of MacKenzie Brook, but I suspect he jigged it.

Luther Corbern

Summer Complaints

There's one thing I've learned in life: us humans always have something to complain about.

In the winter, we're just about always complaining about having to shovel snow all the time, the cold, the short days, the long nights, the water pipes freezing up, the wind, the sleet. Not a wintry night goes by without someone allowing as how he wished it was summer so he could grab his rod and head for the river, smell the lilacs on the warm breezes, plant a little garden, enjoy the birds singing.

When old summer rolls around, the first thing you hear is, "It's too hot! It's too dry! The darn crows woke me this morning at five o'clock! Yesterday when I was weeding the garden, the black flies pretty near eat me up!" I guess it's human nature to not be satisfied.

All this week I've been guiding a fellow by the name of Paul Lambert, a teacher from Worcester, Massachusetts.

Well, us lads might complain a little bit about the weather, the hard fishing, and whatnot, but compared to Paul Lambert, we're like a bunch of salmon sleeping in the cool water at the mouth of Black Brook with Smoky the Bear guarding against poachers.

The other day I heard some kind of a doctor or professor talking on the radio about how every bothersome little thing stays right up there in your head like a bunch of trout you forgot about in your creel. Pretty soon the trout begin to smell so bad that you have to throw them away, creel and all. If you don't throw them away, you're in big trouble.

Stress is what he was talking about. Stress, that accumulation of all the little complaints that individually have no more effect than a single fly bite, but let them hang around and they'll eat you up.

When I was a little boy, I asked a friend of mine, "What do you call those little flies that you can hardly see, the ones that bite so bad?"

"They're midges," he said.

I thought he said midgets and called them midgets all my life. Midgets, I suppose, sounded good enough that no one ever corrected me. My young friend might very well have called them midgets that day long ago, and because no one around here picked me up on the error, for all I know every Miramichier calls them that.

It was never a problem for me, anyway, until I met up with Mr. Paul Lambert.

I was standing with him at the edge of the water, tying on a little No. 8 Smurf, and the midges were threatening to eat me down to the bone.

At one point I rubbed my arms and exclaimed, "Darn midgets! They're crawling all over me!"

"You mean midges," he corrected.

"Yeah," I said. "That's what I said, darn midgets!"

"Haw!" he laughed. "When you say you have midgets crawling all over you, I envision . . . aw, never mind. They're midges. There's no *t* in the word."

"Oh," I said. "I guess you learn something new every day."

A little later, Knob Wilson sailed past us in his canoe and asked me if I'd seen any fish.

"Not many, Knob, old boy," I answered. "Just the one grilt."

"It's Bob, isn't it?" asked Mr. Lambert. "I thought I heard you say Knob."

"You're right, Bob is his name," I said. "But we call him Knob. Did you see his nose? We call him Knob because of his nose."

"And didn't I hear you say you just saw one grilt?" he asked.

"That's right," I answered. "That's all I saw, anyway."

"Well, me too. But it's not grilt, it's grilse."

"Well, if I'd seen two grilts, I'd have told him."

"One grilse, two grilse, half a dozen grilse, it doesn't matter. It's always grilse!" he snapped. "I can't imagine where you people learned to speak English."

We had another little spat when he realized that, for a Miramichier like me, *license* is plural.

A warden checked us one morning.

"You got your license, Luther?" he asked.

"Yes, sir. Here they are. I got them a month ago."

"They? Them? How many fishing licenses did you get, Lute?" asked Mr. Lambert.

"Well, just the one."

For the rest of the week, I clammed up a bit, spoke only when I was directly asked something. I know I have strange ways of saying things, I'm no Oxford graduate. If I was an Oxford graduate I probably wouldn't be guiding for a living. Sometimes I think that when we Miramichiers call a grilse a grilt, midges midgets, and refer to a license as them, it's just a part of our accent, the way we talk. Sometimes I hear other people from other parts of the world say things I know are wrong, but I don't get all upset about it. But then again, I'm not stressed out.

One day, Mr. Lambert sniffed the air, swung to me and said, "Say, Lute, what's that I'm smelling?"

I sniffed the breeze and knew exactly what he was referring to.

"Bamogilia," I said.

"What?"

"Bamogilia. Those trees over there along the shore."

"Well, that's a new tree to me. A very pleasant scent. I guess we don't have them down home."

He was wading waist-deep in the pool and stayed right there in the same spot for what must have been an hour before I heard him say, "Aha!"

I thought he'd hooked into a salmon.

"I figured it out," he yelled to me. "I should have known. What did you call those trees over there?"

"Bamogilia," I said.

"Balm of Giliad!" he yelled. "Balm of Giliad!"

We had seen a fish jump, and he'd been trying for it for quite some time. I was about to tell him to change flies, to try a Cosseboom, but I wasn't sure if I was pronouncing it right. So I said nothing.

At lunch that same day, he yawned and said, "I think I'll have a nap this afternoon. You can go home, Lute. Take the afternoon off."

"How come?" I asked. "I thought you wanted to fish the Firestone Pool."

"Well, I didn't get much sleep last night. A damned woodpecker was hammering on that tin oil drum at the lower end of the camp at five this morning. Craziest bird I ever encountered!"

"Taking the afternoon off is fine with me," I said. "I haven't wed my garden in a couple of weeks."

"You haven't what?"

"I haven't wed my garden," I repeated.

"I think you mean weeded," he corrected.

So, I went home, *weeded* my garden, and came back about six that evening to escort him up to the Firestone Pool where we'd heard there were a few fish taking.

When we met at his camp, I asked, "Have a good nap, Mr. Lambert?"

"Hell, no! I never slept a wink. That woodpecker again. It's there all the time, hammer, hammer, hammer on that old oil drum! And when he's not on the oil drum, he's up on the stovepipe. I spent the whole time trying to figure out why a bird would be pecking on a piece of tin. I think it either thinks that it's a big hollow log with very tough bark and that one day he'll break through and find a treasure of worms and bugs, or it's a territorial thing. Tap-tap-tap-tap-tap — hear how loud I can tap? This is my neck of the woods! I've got the biggest pecker! Haw! But who can say what's going on in the head of a woodpecker? All I know is that he won't let me sleep. There it is now. Hear that crazy woodpecker, Lute? Hammering on the tin."

"Oh. *That's* the bird you're talking about," I said, and right then and there I saw my chance to get a little bit even. "I thought you were talking about a *wood*pecker."

"It is a woodpecker!" he said. "Can't you hear it?"

"Yes, I hear it, but it sounds more like a *tin*pecker to me."

He didn't say a word, just rolled his eyes and sighed.

Well, we went fishing, and he hooked into a salmon and a grilse at the Firestone Pool. He was happy about that, anyway.

The next morning before driving away, he tipped me fifty dollars American, shook hands, and said, "Well, it's been a good week, Lute. It's been too hot, the fishing could've been better, but thanks very much for everything."

"You heading directly back to Worcester today?" I asked.

"That's Wista, Lute. Wista. I'll be in Wista in nine hours, with any luck."

"Good," I said. "Good luck. See ya later."

He was an all right lad, now that I think back on it. I can't complain.

* Log *

August 3

7:15 A.M. One salmon. 15 pounds. Caught by Nean Kooglin's sport, Luke Smith, from Rochester, New York. Caught behind the tractor tire at lower end of pool, on a No. 10 Green Machine.

8:00 A.M. One ~~grilt~~ grilse. 4 pounds. Caught by Lindon Tucker's sport, Neil Dempsy. Caught behind inside car tire, on a No. 10 Butterfly with a green butt.

5:15 P.M. One salmon. 12 pounds. Caught by Paul Lambert from ~~Worcester~~ Wista, Massachusetts. Caught in the Firestone Pool behind the tractor tire, on a No. 10 Butterfly with a green butt.

8:45 P.M. One grilse. 4 pounds. Caught by Paul Lambert. Caught in the Firestone Pool behind truck tire at upper end of pool, on a No. 10 Butterfly with a green butt.

Luther Corhern

A Night on the Cains

Every summer my nephew Hod and I canoe down the Cains for ten miles or so, spend the night at Buttermilk Brook, then continue on home the next day. It's a trip we talk about and look forward to all winter long.

Night is one of my favourite times to be out on the river. If you don't disturb the sand and shore hay, the flies are usually tolerable, and close to the water like that, it's always cooler, just right for sleeping. I usually build a safe little fire in the rocks and watch the stars or their reflection on the water, constellations, airplanes, UFOs, the trees like black fangs against the horizon. Sometimes you'll hear an owl or a coyote, a beaver slapping its tail, a salmon leaping, the mating sound of a cricket from some nearby meadow, perhaps a vehicle man-oeuvring a rocky road in the distance. There's lots of activity, but mostly all is quiet and serene.

A few weeks back, Hod and I ran the Cains again as usual, and everything was so quiet that we found ourselves singing "Old Man River" in sign language so as not to disturb the ambiance.

When we needed to talk, we whispered. That's the kind of lads we are, Hod and me — disturb nothing, leave everything the way nature intended. People who camp and leave their garbage strewn about for the world to see are the worst kind of vermin, in my opinion. The river is where lads like Hod and me spend half our lives. From experience, I've learned that people who litter up the river are either drunk or ignorant or both. But you'd think those people would sober up enough now and again to see the garbage, and you'd think that seeing the garbage would look after the ignorance.

Anyway, Hod and I were on the Cains, and after frying up the few trout we'd caught earlier in the evening, we were sitting in the glow of our little fire, watching the hazy, lazy river, talking about this very thing, when Hod said to me, "Hear that cricket?"

"Yeah," I said. "It's over there in the meadow."

"Sounds like he's desperate or something."

"Sounds like it's in a downright frenzy, if you ask me."

"Lookin' for a little lady, I guess. It must get lonely living way up here. Yep. Yep, I can tell. That old cricket is lonely."

"I never thought of a cricket as being lonely. What makes you think it's lonely?"

"Well, who else but a lonely man would sit in a meadow and play such . . . I don't know . . . such mournful music?"

"You're being anthropomorphic," I said.

"Ah, I don't know about that. What's that mean?"

"Anthropomorphic? Well, it means . . . it's what you call giving human qualities to rocks or trees or moose or crickets. When you talked about that cricket as if it were a man, sitting alone in a meadow pining for a lady, you were being anthropomorphic."

"Hmm. Well, he could very well be like a person. How do we know?"

"Well, for one thing, its brain is no bigger than the head of a pin, and I doubt if it gives much thought to its existence. Everything a cricket does is based on instinct. That cricket doesn't know any other life than the meadow it's in. That meadow is its home."

"Seems a bit too simple to me."

"Well, who knows?"

"Anyway, I love crickets."

"You mean, you appreciate them."

"Yeah, whatever."

"Why don't we skip some rocks?" I suggested.

"Naw. Throw your arm out."

There was a period of silence then, during which Hod sighed a few times, scratched a few itches, whisper-whistled a few bars of "Are you mine rich or poor, tell me darling are you sure . . ." A loon called to us from what sounded like down around the bend, the first loon I'd heard in a long while, and it was good to hear it, good to know there were still a few around.

"Crazier than a loon. Why do people consider loons to be crazy?" asked Hod.

"Because they spend their nights fighting flies on the Cains River, probably," I quipped.

"Ha! Here we are keeping our voices low, trying not to disturb anything, and that old loon is whistling, hooting, and singing like a drunken sailor. Thinks he owns the place."

"In sort of a way, he does own the place," I said.

"Yeah."

"Have you been talkin' to any of the upriver boys lately?" I asked, trying to put the skids under the ennui that seemed to be invading the campsite.

"Not lately. Have you?"

"Oh, yeah. I was at the Old River Lodge the other night, had a chat with Marty Stewart."

"Oh, yeah? How's Marty?"

"Pretty good. Pretty good. Hooked a big salmon, he was telling me."

"That's good. Marty's a good fisherman, all right."

Another long silence. We killed a few mosquitoes and scratched a few bites.

Hod put a stick on the fire, causing sparks to shoot up and disappear into the night. He watched this activity for a minute, then turned to me and asked, "What was that word again?"

"What word?"

"That ant word. Anthra . . .?"

"Anthropomorphic."

"Oh, yeah, anthropomorphic."

"Anyway, Marty Stewart was telling me that that salmon he caught was a pretty strange fish. He said he fished for it for three whole days. He was wading deep, to the top of his waders, and casting as far as he could. And about every half hour or so, the salmon would come for the fly and miss it."

"That happens," said Hod. "They'll do that sometimes when the water is low and warm. Ya gotta cast straight across when that happens, get a little bag in your line, speed the fly up a bit. But you'd think Marty would've known that."

"Oh, Marty knew that trick, all right. But that's what was strange. The water was neither warm nor low, there was a good current, everything. But the salmon kept missing the fly. Marty told me that he must have rolled it fifty times."

"So why didn't he change flies?"

"He did! Tried every fly in his box. But the salmon wouldn't take any of them, just kept rolling for them."

"Yeah, well, that happens."

"Yeah, well, anyway . . ."

"It's getting late. We'll be rising early, I expect. Maybe we should turn in."

"Yeah. I suppose you're right. Something to do, anyway."

So we drowned the fire, said goodnight to the river, crawled into the tent and our sleeping bags. There we lay for the longest time, not saying anything. I don't think either one of us was the least bit tired. Like Hod said, going to bed was just something for us to do. When I think back on it, lying in the total darkness of a tent on a beach of the Cains River doesn't seem like doing very much of anything. We'd been better off watching the fire and the stars. But that's the state of mind we were in, I guess.

After a while, I heard Hod chuckle to himself.

"What?" I asked.

"Oh, nothing. That old cricket is still singing the blues. Hear him?"

"It."

"What?"

"How can you tell it's a him?"

"Well, *it*. You sure know it's summer when you hear a cricket."

"Yeah. Know what I'm thinking about, Hod? I'm thinking about that fish that Marty rolled so many times. You know why it kept missing the fly?"

"No. Why?"

"Well, according to Marty, when he caught it after three days of trying, he looked the fish over before releasing it and discovered that it only had one eye."

"Imagine!"

"Yep. It had gotten hooked in the eye sometime in its past, maybe when it was a parr. Funny, eh?"

"Ha! Makes sense, when ya think about it. Blind in one eye, kept missing the hook."

"Yeah, well, anyway . . ."

"Yeah. Well, good night, Lute."

"Good night, Hod."

There was a long silence, during which all we could hear was the murmur of the river outside our tent. Then once more, closer and louder this time, came the lonesome sound of the cricket. It seemed as though it was right outside the tent

"There's the cricket again," I said.

"Yep. Seems he sneaked up to listen to our conversation."

"Yep."

"Sounds pretty lonesome, doesn't he?"

"We must sound pretty lonesome to him, I think."

"Maybe."

"Have you heard the story about the four men sailing down the river on a marble slab?"

"Yeah. I heard it."

"Oh."

I turned over and listened to the sounds of the night — the river, the loon. A salmon leaped, the cricket sang. Hod mumbled something.

"What's that?" I asked.

"Anthropomorphic."

"What about it?"

"Old Man River . . . is that anthropomorphic?"

"Well, yes, in sort of a way, I guess."

"Well, it seems to me that a cricket is, well, let me put it this way. A cricket is summer personified."

"Ahuh, that too, yep."

* Log *

August 23

As usual in August, there aren't many fish around. We're hoping the full moon tides will change things.

Luther Corhern

All That Glitters

Last summer I guided a wonderful old fellow by the name of Sydney Hammond, from Troy, New York. He was an older man, up in his seventies, I'd say, but he was in very good shape both mentally and physically — cheerful, full of jokes, pleasant to be with. His face was lined in such a way that you knew as soon as you saw him he spent a lot of time smiling, he'd had a good life. Another thing about him was that he had a gold tooth you could see only when he grinned really wide. He said he'd had that tooth put in there on purpose. "It's a tooth especially for golden smiles," he told me.

I liked him a lot.

He stayed at the Salmon Camp for seven days in July during what turned out to be the hottest week we had all year. The water was nearly eighty degrees, and the salmon, as ready to run as a turtle on a fence post, were all hanging out in the cool waters at the mouth of whatever brooks they could squeeze themselves into.

Old Syd never caught a fish all week, but he paid Cavender Bill without complaint. Even tipped me fifty dollars for being, as he put it, "so tolerant with an old man who wants the thrill of catching just one more salmon."

I told him he seemed in good shape and would hook into a good many salmon before he found himself casting upon the Jordan. Next year would be a whole different story.

"Yes, I guess you're right," he said. "Maybe I should plan to come at a different time of year. It used to be that July was a good time to fish the Miramichi, but I know a fellow can't always count on it because of the hot weather. And you don't seem to be getting the runs that you used to. When would you say is the best time to come up here?"

"Well," I said, "if a man had only a week or two to go fishing, I'd head for the river in either late June or sometime in September. The salmon are bigger and tastier in June, but they're meaner in September."

Mr. Hammond took what I told him seriously, I guess, because this year he showed up on the first of September, and Cavender Bill called me in to guide him.

"Yes! I'd be glad to," I said and headed over the hill to the Salmon Camp anxious to greet my old friend.

I hardly recognized him.

He was never a big man, but he looked as if he had lost about thirty pounds. It had been little more than one year since we waved goodbye, but he appeared to have aged ten. His voice was weak, his shoulders drooped, his back was bent — you wouldn't know he was the same man. It turned out he'd been sick half the winter.

"Morning, Lute!" he said. "I'm here for the big one. How's the fishing?"

"Well, sir," I began, but I found myself unable to tell him the truth.

The truth of the matter was that it was the same story all over again. The water was low, and we needed a big three-day rain to get the salmon moving. I found myself having to make the same decision that a great many guides have to make in their careers. And that is, well, I decided to lie.

"The fishing's pretty good," I said. "With any luck, we should hook into a few. How long you stayin' for?"

"Two weeks."

"Well, that's great!" I said. I was glad to hear he was planning to stay. It would be very strange if we didn't get some rain in that length of time. "We'll catch some fish this year."

"If you don't mind, I'd like to fish the Home Pool," he said. "My energy level is not up to par, and I'd sort of like to stick around close to camp."

"That's fine with me," I said.

I rigged up his rod, tied on a little Butterfly for him, helped him into his waders, and we headed for the Home Pool.

As soon as we stepped onto the beach, I knew we were in for hard fishing, because we had the whole pool to ourselves. If Nean or Lindon, if just about any one of the local boys had been there, it would have been a sign that at least a few were running. But to see a pool, especially the Home Pool, empty like that is a sure sign that all the salmon are lying lethargically at the mouths of brooks.

"Go to 'er, Mr. Hammond," I said. "You can't catch 'em with a dry line."

With a sigh that told me he might have guessed the truth, he waded into the river and began to cast. I noticed right away he wasn't casting nearly as far as I'd seen him throw on previous occasions. Not that it mattered that much under the circumstances. But he wasn't even reaching the hot spots.

"It's gonna be a long two weeks," I thought.

Well, I was right in that line of thinking because we didn't get a drop of rain, and the salmon all stayed in the brooks just like I knew they would.

Every day was long and hot, and each one seemed to get a little longer because of the inactivity. And to watch that frail old man beating the water as if every cast was his last didn't make the days any shorter, either. It was enough to make a grown man cry.

Nean, Lindon, and myself were down on the beach skipping rocks across the water one moonlit night, and I brought up the situation, told them the sad tale.

"Two years he's been here and hasn't as much as rolled a fish! What in the name o' God am I to do?"

"We could get a net and sweep the brook, catch him two or three," suggested Lindon.

"Yeah, if the wardens didn't catch us and take our fishing and guiding licenses and fine us more money than we make in the run of a year," says Nean.

"No, you can't take that kind of a risk," says Lindon. "The fact is, Lute, there's not a damned thing you can do. The fish just aren't in the pools right now, and there's nothing anyone can do about it."

"You could take 'im fishing over at the mouth of MacKenzie or down at the mouth of Morris Brook," says Nean. "At least he'd see a few there."

"He'd see a few, all right," I said. "He'd see thousands is what he'd see."

"Well?"

"Well, you know as well as I do that if a warden sees a lad fishing at the mouth of a brook when the weather's hot like it is, he'll know damned well you're there for one reason: jiggin'!"

"Well, ya don't have to jig, do ya?"

"How ya gonna avoid it? There's thousands of salmon in there. There's no way you can throw a hook in there and not catch a fish somewhere, by the tail, by the dorsal fin, in the gills, somewhere. And if you pull a salmon out of the water, foul-hooked like that, you're as guilty of jiggin' as if you intended to do it."

"So what are you gonna do?" asked Lindon.

"I don't know," I said. "Tell him the truth, I guess."

Well, the next morning when I met up with poor old Syd, knowing what I had to tell him and knowing that I should have told him a lot sooner, I was not in one of my better moods. I did not speak more than a word or two to him during the whole walk to the pool.

When we finally got there he sat on a boulder to rest.

"You seem unusually quiet this morning, Lute," he commented.

"Well, yes, I . . . Mr. Hammond, I . . . I have something I
believe I should tell you."

"Yes, Lute? You're not gonna tell me there's no fish in here,
are you?"

"I . . . no, I was just about to say that, well, I . . . we should
maybe go over there to the mouth of MacKenzie Brook and give
it a try."

"Do you think there might be some fish over there?"

"Ah, well, there might be. Maybe we should give it a try."

"You're the guide, Lute. Whatever you say. How do we get
there?"

"I'll canoe us over."

There. I'd done it. And before we as much as got into the
canoe, I was beginning to regret it.

You see, if I should get caught jigging a fish, I'd have to pay
a fine and I'd lose my guide's license, fishing license and job;
that would be one thing. But for this old American gent to get
caught, he'd probably have to pay a much stiffer fine than
mine because he's a non-resident, he'd lose his license, he'd get
kicked out of the country.

But I'd made the commitment and there I was, paddling
like the fit Canadian in a beeline for the mouth of MacKenzie
Brook and to God knows what horrible consequences.

So as not to spook the salmon, I anchored about twenty-
five yards out, moved up, and sat behind Sydney so that the
canoe would hang straight in the current. Then I told him
where to cast.

There was a bit of a breeze on the water, and I don't think
Sydney could see the salmon sleeping in there. But I could see
them as plain as if they were lying right beside me. There were
hundreds of them!

Sydney made a cast, let it swing a bit (the current was very slow), and when he pulled on his line to make cast number two, his line tightened, then went slack again. There was a bit of a swirl and that was all.

"By God, Lute, I tightened up on one!" he exclaimed. "First cast!"

I chose not to comment.

As I knew it would, the same thing happened on his second cast. This time there was a big splash, and I knew he had pricked a salmon's tail.

"There's another one!" said Sydney Hammond.

I looked about guiltily, hoping like hell that no wardens were about. I also listened for any disturbance in the alders or tall grass along the shore. Everything seemed calm and peaceful, sunny and warm, the gentle breeze sparkled on the water — a few birds singing, mosquitoes humming, a chain saw buzzing in the distance. There didn't seem to be any wardens around.

Sydney hooked a salmon again on the third cast. This time, he rolled the fish completely over so that we could see the glitter of its silvery belly. I figured he had it hooked by the dorsal fin. Sydney set the hook, the rod bent, and his reel began to spin.

"I've got him! I've got him!" he yelled. "I think it's a big one!"

"Play it nice and easy," I said. "I'll shove us ashore."

When I pushed the canoe into the mouth of the brook and up onto the shore, I must have spooked a couple of hundred fish. Salmon were swirling and shooting out in all directions.

"Look at all the fish!" yelled Sydney, stepping out of the canoe. "I've never seen anything like it! We should have been fishing here all week."

And that was the problem right there. Now that he saw all

the fish and was hooking them on what he thought was every cast, I'd never be able to get him to fish anywhere else.

I was worrying about this more than anything else when the salmon jumped and revealed itself to be about a ten-pounder. Hooked as it was by the dorsal fin, Sydney had no control over it whatsoever, and thus he thought it was a much larger fish. I couldn't help but grin at the action. And then —

"Lute? Luther, take my rod," said Sydney.

"What's the matter?"

"I don't know . . . got a bit of a pain in my chest . . . need to sit for a spell."

"Here, let me help you," I said, offering him my hand.

"No! No, you play the fish. I don't want to lose it. I fished too hard for it. I'll just sit right here. You land the fish, I'll be all right."

"You sure?"

"Never been better in my life."

So I did as I was told, took his rod and started to play the fish.

I worked at it for several minutes, then looked to see how Sydney was doing.

He was not doing well at all. He was lying on his back, red in the face and gasping for breath. I gave the rod a jerk and broke the leader. Then I ran to the old lad.

I knelt beside him and cradled him in my arms. The sun was shining down on him, and he seemed very warm. I removed my cap and fanned him with it.

"Mr. Hammond . . ."

"It's my heart, Lute . . . I don't have my pills. Did you land the fish?"

"I . . . ah . . . yes, yes. A big one, about twenty pounds."

"Release it?" It was hard to believe that he was thinking of a salmon at a time like that.

"Yeah. You hooked him good," I said. "I let him go."

"Good. We wouldn't want to get caught jigging," he said.

Then he died right there in my arms, a big golden smile on his face.

* Log *

September 1

7:45 A.M. One salmon. 22 pounds. Caught by Sydney Hammond at the mouth of MacKenzie Brook on a number 8 Butterfly.

Luther Corhern

Between Tears and Laughter

Back in 1971, Alden Nowlan, the great Maritime poet, came out with a book called *Between Tears and Laughter*. The title is a poem in itself, four words that describe an abyss I'm sure many of us are familiar with. It's a concept I wish I'd recalled and held onto last Sunday.

Elly, Bill McAfee's wife, passed away about a year ago. Having no children and living quite a number of miles from other family members, Billy was left pretty much alone. Billy loved Elly very much, and her passing saddened him more than most of us, his bachelor friends, could comprehend.

But Billy seemed strong, rarely showed his emotions in any way. Occasionally you'd see him staring blankly at a space only he could envision, sometimes he'd smile ever so slightly and mention her name, refer to something she said or did, but that was about all. No tears. No laughter.

I went to visit him a couple of months ago, and he put his whole state of mind into perspective for me.

"I'm nearly out of my mind with grief," he told me.

"Well, you certainly are good at hiding it," I commented.

"I'm not hiding anything," he said. "To weep is a painful thing to do. It hurts your eyes and throat, gets your nose all out of kilter, even your stomach will get sore from crying a lot. It does nothing for your dignity and self-esteem, either. Nobody wants to hang around with a blubbering idiot.

"What you learn to do is control it, control your emotions. I've learned to cry inwardly, without tears. It's less painful for everyone, including myself. I've also learned to do a whole lot of weeping in a short time. Sometimes I cloud over and whimper, and that's the end of it until the next time."

"So you've learned to do that?"

"Maybe. I mean, I'm not sure if I actually learned to do it. Maybe it's just a natural thing that the human spirit and body adapt to. You know, you get used to something, and all of a sudden it becomes a part of you. Some people get used to living in a messy house or next door to a pulp mill. You see the litter or smell the old mill so much that you don't even know it's there."

"I've always heard that a good emotional breakdown can be good for you," I said.

"Oh, certainly. But you don't need to dwell on it. Remember the old horror movies? One person would enter an abandoned house, and from somewhere within, from upstairs or from the basement, a ghost would eerily laugh or cry. I've been in houses I felt were haunted, but I could tolerate them because I heard nothing. When I lived in that old house down by the river, I occasionally felt the presence of something there, but it was always okay. If I had heard one chuckle or one whimper coming from the walls, I would have left the place quicker than you can say boo."

I'm a bachelor myself and will probably remain that way. Or at least I'm content with my solo existence ninety-nine percent of the time. Yes, it can get lonely, but I generally cover up my emotions in much the same way as Bill McAfee. It's not that difficult for me. I have very little to cry about, and I've never had a handle on how to laugh. At least, most of the time.

Bert Todder, God rest his soul, always believed that for every time you laugh, you cry. Tell him something funny and he'd laugh, "Ha, ha, ha," for a minute or two, then break down and cry because of it, to cancel the laughter out. I think it's an old Dutch practice. Lindon Tucker never learned how to laugh, never found out what syllable to throw into his laughter. Sometimes he'll go, "Tee hee hee," or "Ho ho ho," sometimes he'll go "Yi yi yi yi," you never know what's going to come out of him, how he's going to laugh.

With me, I just grin. I might think your joke is the funniest thing in the world, but all I generally do is grin. As a rule, the most you can get out of me is a little secretive whisper, "Ha!" I'm a comedian's nightmare. You'd get more response from a sleeping cat than from me. Picture it: Bob Hope standing in front of an audience full of people like me. He tells his very best joke, and the whole crowd grins silently, like a bunch of new moons or slits in a milk can.

Silent laughter is not always a bad thing, however. A little grin is hard to interpret, keeps you a bit secretive.

I think Bill McAfee hit the nail right on the head when he said that nobody likes a blubbering idiot. Laughter, on the other hand, can be nice to listen to, like beautiful music. I stress the word beautiful because not all laughter is beautiful, in much the same way that not all music is beautiful. In my opinion, bagpipes and tin whistles should be banned. Play me Celtic fiddle and I leave the room. I feel the same way about somebody laughing a loud, shallow, phoney "Ha ha ha" for several minutes about something that is not very funny. To me, it's disconcerting, embarrassing.

I made a fool of myself last Sunday. I couldn't help it. I lost control. I wince and blush to think about it. I try to reason it out, to be philosophical about it, but nothing helps. I'm a fool. What else can I say?

Last Sunday, my friend Lotty invited me over to dinner.

"Come over," she said. "We're having roast beef. My grandmother will be dining with us. She plays the piano. After dinner we'll gather around the piano and sing."

"Sounds good to me," I said, and on Sunday afternoon I went over.

When I got there, I found Lotty entertaining her mother and father, her brother George, her sister Linda, and her grandmother. Her grandmother is very old, in her nineties, I guessed. She's bright, though, and we had a very interesting conversation over dinner. She had some nice things to say about my grandparents and told me a story about a relative of mine who went to the Yukon in search of gold.

After dinner, we gathered in the living room, and the thin little old woman sat to play. I was expecting "Bringing in the Sheaves," "Rock of Ages," "Faith of Our Fathers," hymns. But instead, "Yankee Doodle went to town, riding on a pony" over and over again. To me, for some reason, it was incredibly funny. The old lady put so much energy into the playing, and the family sang with so much gusto — I can't explain it. At first, inwardly, I was laughing my head off, but all that anyone could detect was my little grin and a barely audible "Ha." They thought it was a grin of appreciation and were so pleased with my response that they sang it again. "Yankee Doodle went to town, riding on a pony . . ."

It was only then, when they hit into it for yet another round, that I lost control. I began to perspire, I turned red in the face, tears began to flow. I tried to swallow the laughter, tried to breathe deeply. I was doomed. I broke down and laughed so hard that they all quit singing just to watch. The grandmother kept right on going, however. "Yankee doodle went to town, riding on a pony, Stuck a feather in his hat . . ."

I became the idiot I detest, laughing long and loud about nothing. It seemed I had saved up all the laughs of my entire life and was releasing the whole lot at that very moment.

"What's so funny?" asked Lotty.

I tried to tell her, "Nothing," but I couldn't wrap my tongue around the word.

"Are you drunk?" asked her brother.

"He's drunk," said her father.

"It's not alcohol," said her mother. "I've seen a good many drunks in my time. He's on something else."

Eventually the laughter collapsed within me, leaving me exhausted. I sat on the sofa, took several deep breaths and tried to think of an appropriate explanation for my behaviour.

With tears in my eyes that could have been tears of sorrow at this point, I said, "I'm . . . I'm sorry, I can't tell you how I enjoy . . . ha ha . . . that tune . . . ha ha ha . . . Yankee ha ha doodle ha ha ha ha."

I should have kept quiet. I was back into it, out of control. I was in a dreadful mess. I couldn't stop laughing no matter how hard I tried. I had gone completely insane, and there was nothing anyone could say or do to help me. As a matter of fact, everything they did or said made it worse. I grew feverish, my scalp began to itch, and even that seemed strange and ridiculous. I finally laughed my way out of the living room, out of the house, and into my old pickup. I laughed until I was nearly home. Then reason entered the picture — cold, stark reality, shame, embarrassment.

It was Tuesday before I worked up the courage to pick up the phone, call Lotty, and apologize.

"I was not drunk or stoned," I told her. "I just lost control, had an emotional breakdown. I don't know why. I'm sorry."

"It's all right," said Lotty. "You're just spending too much time by yourself."

"Well, I . . . I guess there's no sense in dwelling on it," I said.

But I do.

I do.

* Log *

September 15

8:45 A.M. One salmon. 15 pounds. Caught by Elvis Glasby's sport, Leonard Ingalls from Bennington, Vermont. Caught in the Home Pool behind the Bellyview Rock, on a No. 8 Copper Killer.

9:30 A.M. One grilse. 4 pounds. Caught by Cavender Bill. Caught in the Home Pool behind the Furlong Rock, on a No. 6 General Practitioner.

10:00 A.M. Cavender Bill hooked a large salmon but lost it after only a couple of minutes. It was behind the Bellyview Rock and came for the same No. 6 General Practitioner.

3:20 P.M. One salmon. 16 pounds. Caught by Lindon Tucker's sport, Jeff Hogan, from Hartford, Connecticut. Caught on a No. 8 General Practitioner behind the truck tire at the lower end of Firestone Pool.

6:15 P.M. One grilse. 4 pounds. Caught by Nean Kooglin's sport, Lefty Devito from Chicago. Caught in the Home Pool behind the Furlong Rock, on a No. 6 Copper Killer.

Luther Corhern

The Kitchen Table

From its beginning back at Kenny Porter's Spring, the Hemlock Road follows the Miramichi River for about ten miles to where it connects up with Route 8 down at Pitchwood Crossing. From one end to the other, the Hemlock Road has a population of fifty-six people. Louise Walls had a baby last year, so the population increased by more than one percent. It looks like it might drop off this year, however, because poor old Clement Jacobson is nearly a hundred and ailing something awful.

Living on the Hemlock Road, it's not hard to be a reasonably big fish. Nean, for example, is revered from one end of the road to the other for his great singing voice and guitar playing ability. In the eyes of the world, or even the rest of Northumberland County, he would not be considered that great. But on the Hemlock Road, he's the best, a star. My friend Lotty is the best cook, bakes the best biscuits and molasses cookies on the road. Stan Tuney is the best yarn-spinner, Elvis the most sought after fishing guide, Freddy the best barber, Lindon the best fisher-man . . . we all have our little claim to fame. The inhabitants of the Hemlock Road call me the bard because I do a bit of writing, mainly during the fishing season, a daily log for Cavender Bill's Salmon Camp. In the eyes of the literary world, I'm a midge fly, have never gotten any closer to a writer of stature than seeing playwright Norm Foster from across the street in Fredericton. But on the Hemlock Road? I'm the bard.

The funny thing about writing is the questions people ask you.

Take Freddy the barber, for instance. He went to school, learned the trade, set himself up a little shop, hung out a shingle, and people started showing up as surely as hair grows.

You go there, sit in his chair, and allow him to do his job. When he's finished, you either like it or you don't. If you do like his work, you go back to him a month later for another clipping. If you don't like it, you go somewhere else. It's as simple as that. I would think that very few of his customers ask him where he gets his ideas.

When Lotty bakes her biscuits, people might say they're great, or, "Lotty, my dear, you make the best biscuits on the Hemlock Road!" But I doubt if she's ever heard, "You should send that recipe off to *Canadian Living*, Lotty, get it published." Or, "Great biscuits, Lotty! Where do you get your ideas?"

From the time that I was fifteen years old, I always wanted to be a writer. I don't know why, exactly. I guess I thought writers were rich and famous, that they sat in their comfortable offices wielding their mighty pens, captivating the world with all the appropriate words that their wise, creative, and learned minds coughed up. "Get published," I thought, "and you got 'er made."

That concept is as far-fetched as most of the fiction you read. Most writers are poor and lonely people eking out a living under the scrutiny of a cold, ungrateful world. Most of them do it because it's all they can do. I learned this from interviews with various authors on the radio, so although I love to write, I decided to become a fishing guide.

In one interview I listened to, an author explained how he wrote for a year in his hole-in-the-wall office on a novel. It was a good novel, he thought, so he began sending it to publishers. Every time he sent the manuscript off, it cost him an average of eight dollars in postage. With the manuscript, he sent a self-addressed stamped envelope, another eight dollars. He did this for months and months, even years, before he finally found a publisher who considered his work right for the company. Then came the promotional tour, and he found himself travelling all over eastern Canada (the publisher paid for meals, hotel rooms and mileage) signing books and reading from his work. Six months after the publication date, he received his royalty cheque for $1700. That book was short listed for the Commonwealth Writers Prize, won the Thomas Raddall Award for best fiction in Atlantic Canada, and is being read and studied in schools and universities throughout the Maritimes. The interviewer introduced him as a "well-known author" and referred to his novel as "a classic."

The best thing about the interview, though, was when the interviewer asked the author where he got his ideas.

"I don't know," said the author. "From reading perhaps, from life's experiences maybe, from the muse. I'm not sure."

I bet "Where do you get your ideas?" is a question every author gets asked at one time or another. Even I, the bard of the Hemlock Road, got asked it the other night.

I'm a fishing guide, not a real author. All I started off to write is a little Salmon Camp log. Not much happens, and thus there's not much to write about. At first, this presented me with a bit of a problem. Then, because I always wanted to be a writer, I decided to turn the log into something else. I began to embellish, to lie like the devil. If Lindon Tucker catches a grilse, I write it down as a monstrous salmon. If Cavender Bill catches a fish, it's frequently bigger than anyone else's — he *is* my boss, and I figure it's good public relations to make him feel good. I throw in a bit of humour, a few jokes, anything that will spruce it up a bit, make it a better read. Because I only have about six readers, it doesn't really matter what I write. Nobody cares, everybody knows the truth anyway, and it's all in fun. I read the log aloud to Lotty, Cavender Bill, and the boys every now and again just to hear them laugh.

In my last log, I wrote a bunch of lies about the time I shot a great blue heron for Thanksgiving dinner, about how I shot it from across the river and sent my little American cocker spaniel to fetch it, about how comical it was to see that little dog swimming the river with that big long bird trailing behind her. "It was not bad eating," I wrote. "The drumsticks were a foot long."

I read the story to them down at the Salmon Camp the other evening, and they all thought it was the very best of a yarn. That made me feel good. Hearing them laugh is all the reward I want for my writing.

Anyway, I think it was Stan who swung to me and asked, "Where do you get your ideas, Lute?"

I remembered the radio interview with the author and how he'd had some difficulty in answering the question. If the author had given it any thought, he would have answered it as quickly and as truthfully as I did. You see, there is a place where ideas come from. It's the most popular place on the Hemlock Road, in New Brunswick, even in the Maritimes. It's where we eat and drink and party, talk and play games, argue and laugh; it's where we do our income tax returns and figure out where our next meal is coming from; it's where we read our morning papers, do our crossword puzzles, roll our coins, plan our futures, and design our gardens, sheds and barns; it's where we decide to become barbers and fishing guides; it's where we write our letters, poetry, books, and logs. The place where most of my ideas come from is the place where I do just about everything.

I turned to Stan and answered his question in three words. "The kitchen table," I said.

* Log *

October 12

2:15 P.M. One salmon. 38 pounds. Caught by Cavender Bill in the Ramp Pool on the Wreath on a No. 6 General Practitioner.

5:30 P.M. I caught a ten-pounder on the Wreath in the Ramp Pool. It came for a No. 8 Micky Finn.

Note: 186 fish were taken in Cavender Bill's pools this year. That's 42 more than last year. Things are looking up.

Luther Corhern

The Cure-All

My grandmother lived with us when I was a boy. She was a clean-living Baptist, and the rest of us were Anglicans. My grandmother thought that the Anglican organization was a bit too Catholic for her liking. We rarely crossed ourselves, but she had an idea that we were doing it behind her back. "You can't trust anyone but a Baptist," she used to say. She also always wanted to eat red meat on Friday. She suspected that the practice of eating fish on Friday was some sort of Catholic conspiracy, a plot to try and convert her. It didn't matter to her (or perhaps she just didn't realize) that nine out of ten Fridays we had nothing else in the house to eat but fish. On every other day of the week my grandmother would eat salmon, trout, mackerel, shad, smelts, whatever fish we could come up with, and enjoy it, even praise it, even thank the Lord for his generous bounty. But because she believed the Catholics would only eat fish on Friday, she would not.

"Eat fish on Friday? Next thing you'll have me kneeling in church! Bring on the beef!"

We were brought up on fish. If it were not for fish, I would probably not be sitting here writing. We ate fish, fished fish, smoked and salted fish, and showed other people where to fish. We bought our clothing with the money we collected for allowing people to fish our pool. We even used fish — salt herring — for medicinal purposes. I don't know what the ailment was, but I recall my mother putting salt herring on my sister Lena's feet to absorb the fever.

Several times a year the Baptist minister, Reverend Ralph Kamp, dropped in to visit my grandmother to assist her in trying to convert us Anglicans. "Big, fat, and good looking," was how my grandmother described him. I remember a few things about him, that he was indeed quite fat, wore dark-rimmed glasses and a green and black checked suit. I remember, too, that he could ad lib the most profound and elegant prayers at the drop of a hat, and that he would never leave the premises without eating. He'd come in time for lunch, and if he missed lunch, he'd hang around for afternoon tea. Sometimes my mother would put the tea and cake on as soon as he arrived just to get rid of him, because if he didn't get his tea and cake, he'd stay for supper.

Back in 1958, we were exceptionally poor. My father was working in the woods for a contractor from Doaktown, but the snow was so deep and the weather so cold that he rarely reached any kind of a decent scale. He'd stay in a camp twenty-three miles up in the woods five nights of the week, come home on Friday evening, dirty and coughing kerosene and wood smoke from his lungs, and give a cheque to my mother, a cheque barely large enough to pay the hydro bill or buy the boots that I, or perhaps Lena, so desperately needed. My mother would spend all weekend washing his clothes, delousing him, and getting him ready for Sunday afternoon, when he climbed on the back of a truck with eight or ten other men for the cold and windy ride back into the woods. Because I was too little to do much, my father would spend his weekends splitting wood and cleaning the barn, pitching down hay from the mow, doing all he could to make life a bit easier for my mother.

It was after one of those weekends, on a Monday, that Reverend Kamp showed up.

Lena was sick in bed with a fever, the salt herring on her feet. My mother, perhaps afflicted with the same ailment as Lena, should have been in bed, too, but there were the fires to keep burning and the cattle, the hens, and now perhaps even a preacher to feed. Such were the demands on my mother that she allowed me to stay home from school that day, and though I was more often in her way than not, I helped her to the best of my ability.

We were in need of things, flour, eggs (the hens were not laying at that time of the year), sugar, salt, beans, soap, tea, aspirin, basic things, but my mother was just too ill, and it was much too cold for her to attempt to walk the mile and a half to the nearest store. I was too young, my grandmother was too old, and Lena was up in her room with the salt herring on her feet. Not a pretty picture.

Reverend Kamp arrived at noon.

"And how's Mrs. Corhern today?" he asked my grandmother.

"I'm not too well, Reverend," she answered. "I have a sore back, corns on my feet, and, and, and look at the back of my hand, would ya?"

The Reverend looked at the bruise on the back of Grandmother's hand.

"Well well well," he commented.

"I hit that on something or other," she said. "Don't even remember doing it. Would you pray for me, dear Reverend Kamp? For me" — she gestured at my mother and me — "and them."

"Surely," said the Reverend and slid to his knees. So did my grandmother, so did my mother, and so did I. It always puzzled me why Reverend Kamp kneeled to pray in our kitchen but thought it unnecessary to do so in church.

Reverend Kamp did not just pray. For the next hour, or what seemed like an hour, he preached an entire sermon. He asked the Lord to cure my grandmother's many afflictions; he asked Him to bless poor Fred and Kate, little Luther and Lena, and encourage them to enter into the true faith, to accept the poor lost lambs into His flock. He asked for guidance into this frustrating and complicated matter. Then he talked about the

161

Premier of Quebec (I forget the issue) and an unnamed mayor of an unnamed town, who was thought to be perverted in some way or another, "best left unspoken, unuttered in the presence of innocent ears." He covered yields and bounties, icy roads, drinking, sins of the flesh and of the soul, saints and rakes, lambs and lions. Then, last but not least, he elaborately plunged into the subject of money and how so much more of it should be given to the church.

"Amen."

"Amen."

"Amen!"

"Amen."

The sweetest word in the world.

"Now," said my grandmother, "I think you should go up and speak with poor little Lena."

The look of horror on my mother's face told me that Lena's room had not been tidied up, that Lena was sick and perhaps sleeping, that Lena had salt herring on her feet.

"Oh, it would be my pleasure," said Reverend Kamp. "The poor lamb, yes, of course."

Well, it was unavoidable, there was nothing my mother could do but proclaim a hundred apologies for the state of Lena's room and lead the way up. My grandmother, Reverend Kamp, and I followed her up the creaking stairs to Lena's room. We found Lena pale and dishevelled. Her room smelled of Vicks, Sloan's, and salt herring.

We all knelt again, and Reverend Kamp went into his second sermon, shorter but no less elaborate than the first. I don't think poor Lena had a clue what was happening or what was being said. She looked about with clouded eyes, moaned now and again, and occasionally grinned, sighed, cooed, whimpered, and hacked.

Halfway through, my mother started to cry, and I saw the

look of satisfaction and victory on the faces of my grandmother and Reverend Kamp. I suppose he was thinking that
he had broken through, that he had finally penetrated the
stubborn walls of my mother's cold and sinful heart. The funny
thing about it was that I think my mother was so exhausted she
would have encouraged and nourished the concept if only he
would get up, shut up, and leave.

After the prayer, Reverend Kamp asked, "What's with the
herring?"

My already sick and perspiring mother blushed and coughed
into her hand. "Salt herring," she said. "On the feet like that.
S'pose to be good for the fever."

"Indeed. Never heard of that."

"Oh, yes," my grandmother put in, "the only cure. Draws
the fever, it does. Saved many a child, salt herring."

"Well, I'll be! I've heard of cod liver oil being good for you,
but salt herring on the feet . . ."

"Yes, yes. Bless us and save us, yes."

"Well, I'm sure she's going to be just fine," said Reverend
Kamp, smiling down on Lena. "Keep her warm, give her aspirin,
she'll be fine."

Back downstairs in the kitchen, my mother said, "Well,
Reverend, thanks for coming."

"My pleasure," said the Reverend and sat by the table. "The
work of the Lord is my business. I make my rounds as often as
I can."

I heard his belly growl.

So did my mother.

"You must be hungry," said my grandmother. "Fix the man
something to eat, Kate."

"Oh, don't go to any trouble, dear woman. A cup of tea,
perhaps. Maybe some little thing to eat, not much, mind you.
Don't go to any trouble."

"Well, I didn't get to the store today," said my mother. "We're all out of tea, I'm afraid."

"Oh, well, that's quite all right. Anything at all."

"The store is a long way off, and it's so cold outside, too cold to walk, and I've not been feeling well."

"Well, don't you worry about it. I don't need tea. Anything at all for me. A glass of milk, perhaps, and a piece of cake or something. Don't worry about it. I'm not all that hungry. Anything at all."

"Fix the man something, Kate."

"Well, I suppose I could. I could peel a few potatoes and . . . do you like salt herring, Reverend?"

The Reverend Kamp hesitated, then checked his watch.

Luther Corhern

The Craziest Dreams

Boys! I've been having bad nightmares lately! I get them every winter, but they've never been as scary as they are this year. They're what you might call recurring dreams, I guess. They have to do with the opposite sex and marriage.

I dream I meet up with the nicest little lady you ever laid your eyes on and we get married. I carry her across the threshold of my trailer. She's a woman with substance; a woman with money; she's tall and blonde and beautiful. She has eyes like Elizabeth Taylor's, and they gaze upon me with love and admiration. She rubs me in all the right places to make me feel whole, contented, warm inside. She cooks up a storm, plants flowers, cleans and organizes my trailer — everything from my fly boxes to my waders, from my golf balls to my three wood, from my chewing tobacco to my whittling knife are in their rightful places. I have to convert my junk shed into a closet to accommodate the suits and ties she buys me.

I like to plant things haphazardly, a clump of potatoes here, a beet patch there, a cucumber patch at one end of the trailer, and a radish bed where the barn used to be. But in my dreams, all that changes. In my dreams, everything is planted in neat, straight-as-an-arrow rows. In my dreams, even the fiddleheads in the gully grow in straight-as-an-arrow rows.

In my recurring nightmare, I get up in the morning and get all cleaned up before I have coffee and do the crossword puzzles, instead of the other way around. She kisses me before I go over the hill to fish and again when I get home. She kisses me after I eat and head out to the golf course and when I get home again. She kisses me after dinner as I head back to the river to fish until dark.

And when we go to bed at night, she . . . well, I won't get into that.

Shad Nash almost got married once. He came within an inch, one little word of acquiring matrimonial bliss. "I asked a woman to marry me and she said no," he told me. "A close call."

Because of his experience, his close encounter, I thought I'd confide in him about my nightmares. Monday morning, I woke up in a sweat, and, soon as I got around to it, I drove over to Shad's place. I found him in the kitchen, playing the banjo.

I bared my soul to him.

"It's getting so I hate to go to bed at night," I told him. "What will I ever do?"

"It's not good, Lute," he said. "Not good at all. It sounds to me like you might need to see a shrink, a whatchamacallit, a psychiatrist." Here he plucked the strings of his banjo for effect.

"It's that bad, eh?"

"Oh, yes. There's no doubt in my mind. There's some pretty shady stuff swimming around in your head. You could be in serious trouble."

"What do you think a psychiatrist could do for me, Shad?"

"Lie. Psychiatrists mostly lie to you, to make you feel better."

"I could get a politician to do that."

"But you'd *know* the politician was lying. You need a psychiatrist, a good liar."

"Know any psychiatrists, Shad?"

"Well, you'd find one in Saint John, no doubt."

"That's a long drive, and he'd charge me a lot of money, wouldn't he?"

"You got that right. And you'd need an appointment. You might not get to see him until next summer."

"Bad time to be psychiatristing."

"Yeah, you'd better think of something else. How about Stan Tuney?"

"Stan Tuney!"

"Stan's the biggest liar I know. He can tell you anything at all, and half the time you can't help but believe him. Make a good psychiatrist, Stan would. And you don't ever need an appointment. Take a pint with ya and his door is always open."

"Hmm. Stan, eh?"

"Go see Stan."

So that evening I picked up a pint of Seagram's and over to Stan's I went.

"I have a problem, Stan," I confessed, and proceeded to tell him about my dreams.

"That's not a serious problem," he said. "Why are you letting a little dream bother you?"

"Well, it's not just the dreams," I said. "I could deal with the dreams if I could just stop thinking about them when I'm awake."

"Who's the woman in your dreams?"

"Nobody you know."

"Lotty?"

"No, not Lotty. If it was Lotty, I could handle it."

"In your dreams, does this woman want to fish with you?"

"No, not that I recall."

"Does she go golfing with you?"

"No, I don't think so."

"Well, it don't sound too bad."

"But it is bad, Stan. I'm sick, I tell ya. It's not natural for a man to think about getting married, is it?"

"Oh, come now, Lute! Don't be naive. Every man thinks of marriage now and again."

"They do?"

"Of course they do. It's perfectly natural."

"Then why does it bother me so much?"

"Because you're not putting it into perspective. You have to think about what's real and what's not. It has to do with ideals."

Stan Tuney, the master liar.

"Have a drink, Stan, and tell me more."

"Ideals are like . . . are like the hairline. They recede with middle age. Mid-life is what's happening to you, Lute. Amid the turmoil of mid-life a few dreams, ideals, regrets, fantasies are leaping out of your subconscious, like frogs from pond to pond. Don't worry about it. It'll only happen for a while, then reality will return."

"If I only knew what the reality was."

Stan yawned and scratched his belly. If I hadn't known him so well, I might have thought he was bored. But I know him very well. When Stan yawns and scratches his belly, it means he's thinking, fabricating, conjuring up new lies.

"Now, you say this girl in your dreams is young and pretty?"

"Yes, sir."

"And you say she's a great cook and neat and tidy, organized and loving, that in bed at night she . . ."

"Yes, all of that."

"Well, you're pretty much of a slob, right, Lute?"

"Well, I . . . a bit of a slob, I suppose."

"And you're not much to look at."

"I'm a . . . I suppose you're right."

"And you guide for a living."

"Correct."

"And you snore at night and make various other crude noises in the morning."

"Well . . ."

"You fish from sunrise to tee-off time and golf from tee-off time to evening fishing time, taking a break for bodily functions only."

"Pretty close."

"Well, there's the reality, Lute. This woman might exist in your dreams, but no woman in her right mind would have the likes of you around, not in her wildest dreams. And if there's any woman out there who would consider the likes of you, you can bet that she is crazier than the proverbial loon — in which case you'd be wise to stay clear of her."

"Thanks a lot, Stan. You're absolutely right. Thanks. You've made me feel so much better. Gave the old ego a boost, you did. Thanks a lot."

"Don't mention it, Luther, my boy. Go home and enjoy your dreams."

Taking Stan's advice, I went home. And I did dream about her, time and time again. Hell! I think I'm in love.

Good racket!

Luther Corburn

Thirsts of the Soul

A fast gun for hire, a soldier of fortune, a champion, a paragon of knighthood; his symbol the horse's head, the chess piece; a gentleman living in a swank hotel in San Francisco; a hard hitter with an expensive pistol and a hidden derringer — Paladin, of *Have Gun Will Travel*. In the early sixties, when I was a little boy, Paladin the bounty hunter, the vigilante dressed in black, was my hero.

Cowboy was our favourite game back then, and our barn was where we played it. There were cows and horses in our barn, so we actually did smell like cowboys, not that I remember our odour ever being an issue. We didn't ride the big old draft horses and we didn't rope and hog-tie the cattle, but we were all under the same roof, and somehow they were as much a part of the game as us boys were. I suppose they supplied the sound effects. It was all imagination anyway. If I, with a piece of board sawn to look like a gun on my hip, could be Paladin, our old mares with the dung balls on their hips were as good as the sleekest, blackest alpha stallions that ever galloped upon the western plains.

In 1960, my favourite line was, "Okay boys, I'm about to introduce you to the rough and tumble." I don't know where I got the line. Picked it up in a comic book, on TV, from Paladin maybe. In the barn, while watering and feeding the cows and horses, my father must have heard me say that line just about every day we played there. He would have heard "Bang! Bang! Bang! Ping! You missed!" a good many times as well.

Yelling out "Ping! You missed!" was how my friend George managed never to get hit. You could be ten feet away from him, aim a cap gun straight at him, and yell "Bang!" Even if there was no boulder or door hinge or anything else handy to him for the bullet to hit and ricochet from, George would immediately yell "Ping! You missed!" I suppose he figured that if your gun fired make-believe bullets, he could conjure up a make-believe object for your bullets to glance from. Sometimes even at point blank range, with the muzzle of your cap gun pointed directly into his back or belly, he'd yell "Ping!"

"How'd that happen?" you'd ask.

"You hit my belt buckle" — or silver dollar, or gold watch — he'd say. There was no way you could gun him down.

In 1960, all I wanted for Christmas was a toy derringer like the little one that Paladin of *Have Gun Will Travel* always kept hidden somewhere on his person. Putting it into perspective, it wasn't much to ask for. Other kids wanted dolls and skates, skis and trucks, wagons, hockey sticks, chemistry sets, microscopes, bicycles, books, and clothes. But me? A derringer. The one I wanted was displayed in the toy section, page thirty-one of the Eaton's Christmas Catalogue.

I wrote a note much like the following:

Dear Santa,

    I've been a good boy all year. All I want for Christmas is a derringer. You'll see it at the bottom of page 31 of the Eaton's Christmas Catalogue, number 29038-62, $3.95.

                Yours truly and thank you very much,

                      Luther Corhern

I gave the note to my mother. My mother always put our notes to Santa in the oven of our kitchen range. Santa or one of his elves would find them there sometime during the night after everyone was in beddy-bye land. We didn't have a fireplace at our house, so Santa always had to come down our stovepipe and out through the oven in order to pick up our notes and deliver our gifts.

Santa Claus dealt directly with the T. Eaton Company and the Post Office Department in those days. We'd write our letters to Santa, and a few weeks before Christmas, my father would go to the post office and return with a box, always from Eaton's, but somehow, too, everything within was always from Santa. Mail, including our box from Eaton's, was delivered to the post office by train. In this way, according to my father, Santa didn't have to carry so much in his sack, saved wear and tear on the reindeer.

About two weeks before Christmas, 1960, a box the size of a refrigerator arrived at our house. I assumed a derringer was in it.

I was ten years old in 1960, a thin, scrawny, spoiled kid with a whole bunch of imagination and a curiosity great enough, almost, to be harmful and dangerous. I'm still curious. I can never leave well enough alone. But in 1960, what can I say? I was a boy.

Now, the box the size of a refrigerator had many gifts in it. Hopefully the derringer was in it, too. I wasn't sure. I had seen the little thing in the catalogue, and I'd written to Santa about it. But I couldn't help but wonder if it really came or not. I also felt a burning need to see what it looked like, to hold it in my hand. It was two weeks before Christmas, and two weeks was a very long time. My mother had placed the box in her bedroom, right there in the corner where I could see it every time I just happened to go in. And it was funny how many times I felt I needed to enter my mother's bedroom during those days. I'd come home from school and select my mother's room to do my homework in. "The lighting's better there," I told my mother. "And it's so private."

"But it's not private," she reasoned. "You can hear every noise in the house from up there."

"I like to hear the radio while I work," I told her. "You play the radio while you prepare supper, right?"

"Yes, but . . ."

"I like to listen to the Christmas songs while I work in your room, in your well-lighted and private room. Just yesterday I heard "O Come All Ye Faithful" while I was up there doing a math problem, and it all worked out so much easier for me. I felt kind of like Einstein. There's nothing like a good background choir to bring out the genius in a person."

"Yeah, well, stay away from the big box."

"Oh, sure, Mom. Sure."

"If I see that you've been tampering with the box, I'll send whatever it is you want for Christmas back to Santa," she warned. "So leave it alone."

I remember the box was surprisingly light for the size of it. One day, while graphically analyzing a paragraph from my English text, with Gene Autry's voice singing "Up on the House Top" coming from the radio in the kitchen, I learned, quite by accident, that I was able to tip the box over so that it rested on its side. I also learned that there was a little crack in the bottom of the box right where the flaps joined. I was curious about that. Another curious thing about the box was that it was very dark inside. You couldn't see a thing in there without a flashlight. Even with a flashlight, I found I couldn't see much. What I really needed, I learned, was a bigger crack.

Now, a derringer is such a tiny thing. And it did not seem to be at the bottom of the box. I could see other things, a sweater, a tie, a big pair of gloves, a scarf, what could have been a lamp . . . but no derringer.

The crack where the flaps joined at the top of the box was covered with strips of tape. Nice tape, but too much of it, I thought. I removed some of it. Just a bit. Just enough so that I could see with the aid of a flashlight that my sister was going to get the doll she wanted. I could see another box big enough to accommodate a pair of boots or skates, but nothing that looked like it might have a derringer in it.

On another day, while I was studying for a geography exam and listening to Bing Crosby singing "Jingle Bells," I noticed that the corner of the big box had somehow gotten damaged. Not a big tear, but big enough to peep through, if you were so inclined. You could see right in . . . with a flashlight.

But you couldn't see a tiny derringer, of course.

Through other damaged parts of the box, through other holes in other corners, I learned what everyone in the family was getting for Christmas, but never did I accidentally stumble upon a little *Have Gun Will Travel* derringer.

A couple of days later, while I was into some serious studying, my mother came into her room and seemed amazed to find that the box had been damaged a bit here and there.

"Did you do that?" she asked pointing at a hole in one of its corners.

"Me? Now, you know me better than that, Mom!"

"Then how did it get torn?"

"Mice, I suppose."

She hid the big box, put it in the closet and locked the door. She put the key next to her bosom. I told her it wasn't necessary, that I would trap the mice, but Mother insisted, locked it away.

"Well, I tried," I said to myself. "Now what?"

The next day I said to my mother, "Know what, Mom? Donald Keenan is getting a derringer for Christmas, too. I think it's the same as the one I asked for."

"What in the world is a derringer?" she asked.

"You know, the little gun I want for Christmas."

"My goodness, Luther! Why didn't you tell us you wanted a little gun for Christmas?"

"I did, Mom! I did! I told you three weeks ago! I wrote it in my note to Santa!" Her insinuation crushed me. Had I forgotten to tell them? Had they forgotten? Had Santa received my note? It seemed to me that I had given the big box a thorough examination.

"So what am I getting for Christmas?" I tried in a casual, conversational way.

"I can't tell you that, dear. You want to be surprised on Christmas morning, don't you?"

"Yeah, yeah, I forgot what I was asking. A good thing you didn't slip it out. To know would spoil everything."

Then Mother said something that threw me off the scent. She said, "We got you something, dear, and I know you're really going to like them."

Them.

Them?

A derringer could not be referred to as a *them*. A derringer was a single item. *Them* is plural. Did this mean they really hadn't purchased a derringer? Did they maybe get me a bag of marbles instead? Could I expect to awaken on Christmas morning and open a gift to find perhaps a bag of plastic toys that no kid in his right mind would be caught dead playing with?

Them. I tried to picture what *them* could be. A pair of something, perhaps. Mitts? Socks? *Them* sounded like clothing. *Them* suggested sunglasses, coloured pencils, ear muffs, skates, two or more books, a box of chocolates, a lunch box and thermos, things, plural, two front teeth, not a derringer.

Sleepless nights is what her reference to *them* caused me. I didn't want a *them*. I wanted one, singular, a derringer that I could hide in my sneaker or pocket or just about anywhere at all, and someday, when Donald or George or Franky or who-ever least expected it, just when he thought he had the jump on me, I'd pull the tiny gun, and — "Bang! Bang! Bang!" — the whole lot would be vanquished by none other than Luther Corhern.

Luther *Have Gun Will Travel* Corhern and his single-unit, not-a-*them* derringer. I envisioned George shooting me at point blank range and me yelling, "Ping! You hit my derringer!"

My mother was a very smart woman, a superior intellect. She was always smarter than me. Still is. She knew all about me, knew what I was up to. She knew I'd been on the trail like a bloodhound on a still day, and she knew I would not give it up. My mother knew more about me, my imagination and curiosity, the hungers and thirsts of my soul, than I did. She had deliberately used the word *them* to throw me off, and it had worked magnificently. Not only that, she had used the word *them* and hadn't lied.

On Christmas morning, I opened a box big enough to accommodate a pair of skates. Fumbling with the ribbon and the paper, I thought, "Too big for a derringer." I had a lump in my throat because I distinctly remembered emphasizing that a derringer was what I wanted. I did not feel greedy or selfish in any way for my humble request. I did not think it unreasonable for a boy ten years old to expect one tiny, inexpensive little toy gun for Christmas. I had tossed the concept around to the point of preoccupation and couldn't understand the principle behind not getting it, behind getting something she referred to as *them* instead. I knew that my sister was getting pretty much what she wanted. I knew this from accidentally peeping into the big box the size of a refrigerator. Why not me? Had I been a bad boy? Was I not loved? And there I was opening a box big enough to put a pair of skates in, a box big enough to house a *them*, a box big enough to house twenty-five derringers.

The moment it took me to open that gift was an important one, maybe one of the most important moments of my life. I say this because it was nearly forty years ago and I remember it as if it had occurred yesterday. I remember the tree with its shabby decorations, the gentle snowstorm beyond the window, the ribbons and wrapping paper strewn about the room, the sudden lull of activity, all eyes on me.

In the box was a black leather gun belt with two holsters, two beautiful cap guns with white plastic handles, and just above the right holster was a tiny pocket. A derringer exactly like the one I wanted was in the little pocket. Also in the box was a little wallet with about twenty-five calling cards that read, "Have Gun Will Travel."

Yes, it was an important moment. To weep with joy is not something that often occurs in a person's life.

Luther Corbern

Trailer Fever

I like the winter, don't you? Lots of time to get your jigsaw and crossword puzzles looked after. I like shovelling snow and freezing my buns off getting my old truck started, too. I have friends who go to Florida or Mexico every year to avoid the cold weather. Wimps!

What do you think was going through our forefathers' heads when they chose this location to move to a hundred and some years ago? The nice winters? The cool, slushy springs that smell like dog turds? The mosquitoes and black flies in the summers? The autumns, no doubt. There's so much to look forward to in the autumn. In the winter my neighbourhood is so over-crowded with rich Floridians and Mexicans you can hardly find a place to park your car. They come here for the winter to get away from the old warm breeze and sunshine.

The other day, the temperature rose to about ten below, and the wind came up and brought the clouds with it, a solid, emery-grey blanket of clouds that told me we were in for a blizzard.

Not wasting any time, I jumped into my old pickup and wheeled her into the village, stocked up on provisions, hurried home again, carried in enough wood to last three days, checked the insulation wrap on my water pipes, placed my snowshoes within easy reach of the door, and settled in. I had my food and drink, my wood, my television, half a dozen paddles that needed more whittling and sanding, and some good tobacco.

"Let 'er come," I said to myself. "I'm ready."

By five o'clock, darkness had fallen, the wind had increased to fifty miles per hour, and the snow was shooting past my window like so many little arrows. The wind shook my old trailer with every gust, and at times I thought I was going to be swept right over the hill and into the river.

After supper, I turned on the TV and heard Rose, the weather woman, quite safely declare there was a chance of snow.

By noon the next day, we had fourteen inches more of the white stuff with no sign that the storm was about to do anything other than get worse.

When I was a kid, I used to like a storm. In the middle of it all, I'd find myself fantasizing about being snuggled down in warm, cozy dens with little furry animals.

A little boy can do that.

A man can do that to a certain extent if he hasn't completely forgotten the little boy he used to be. But after a day or so, a man tends to get restless. Especially if the electrical power goes off like it did all over our area on Sunday afternoon.

Alone in a candlelit trailer, you can dream about fishing in a great pool on a perfect day or fantasize about little furry animals for only so long. Then you fall into a monotonous routine that soon has you pacing and talking to yourself. I spent most of Sunday afternoon walking from one room to another, eating, drinking, smoking, eating some more, stoking the fire. I bet I walked from the refrigerator to the stove thirty times. By the time six o'clock rolled around, suppertime, I was too full to eat. I tried whittling, but I just didn't have the heart to work on something as summery as a paddle on such a miserable day.

I started going to the door, opening it, watching the storm. My old pickup appeared to be nothing more than a mound of snow.

"Could a man survive in such a storm?" I asked myself. "If the trailer caught on fire, or the roof caved in, could I make it to Nean's place, or down the road to Lindon's? Could a man chance crossing the river on the ice to hole up at Elvis Glasby's or Stan Tuney's?"

At about six-thirty, I grabbed a deck of cards and started playing solitaire at the kitchen table. I must have played twenty games without a win. When I got bored with solitaire, I tied flies for a while. I even invented a fly, a little white one with a sky-blue body, a fly I thought would work well on a day that was mostly clear but with a few fluffy white clouds around. At about seven-thirty I thought I'd read something and was going through the magazines I keep under my mattress when I was startled by a knock on my door.

Thinking that someone must be in trouble, I hurried to the door and opened it to encounter Lindon Tucker, looking like a bedraggled snowman. I don't think I would have been able to identify him if it hadn't been for his grin, his missing cuspids.

"Come in, Lindon, come in. What in the name of God brings you out on such a night?"

He unstrapped his snowshoes and stood them beside mine. "It's not so bad," he said, stepping inside and brushing himself off.

"Not so bad! There must be two feet of snow down!"

"Yeah, yes sir, yep, two feet, maybe more. Oh, ah, I thought I'd just see how you were gettin' along. Oh, ah, I was ah, I was patchin' me waders, and, well, I ran out of patchin'. Was wonderin' if ya had any to spare."

"Patchin' your waders! It's New Year's Eve!"

"Yeah, well, oh, ah, t'weren't much else to do. The weather's not so bad, could be worse, and besides, I was starting to climb the walls." He hauled a half-empty pint of Golden Anchor rum from his pocket and handed it to me. "Thought I might trade you this for the patchin'." He grinned when he said this, and I understood where he was coming from.

"Well, take your coat off and have a seat. To tell you the

truth, I was half thinking about goin' to visit someone, myself. Thought I might even try to make it over the river to see Stan."

"Well, ya won't have to go over the river, because Stan's headin' over here soon's he feeds the horse. Should be here any minute. I was just there."

"You crossed the river in this storm?"

"Oh yeah, yep. Crossed 'er, I did. Over and back. Only one air hole and that's down in front o' Nean's. Stepped right along, I did. Wind pretty near blowed me away, but I kept 'er to my back. No trouble. This trailer's nice and warm, eh? That old house o' mine is colder than a barn. Should get myself a trailer, I should. In this country, a man has to be crazy to live in a house."

I poured us drinks from his bottle and was just about to sit down for a chat when, sure enough, Stan Tuney showed up.

"What brings you out on such a night?" I asked.

"Well, I was just glancing through the Orvis catalogue and came upon this nice nine-footer. Thought I might order it. I don't need a new fishing rod, of course, but ya can always do with a spare. You have one like it, and I thought I'd get your opinion."

"It's a good rod," I said. "You're paying a lot for the name, though."

"Yeah, well. Get your patchin', Lindon?"

"Not yet, not yet. No hurry. Gonna be lots of shovelling after this storm's over."

"I'm not shovelling until the plows go. No sense shovelling until the plows go. They just throw it all right back into your driveway," said Stan.

"Well, I'm lucky to have the plow on the front of my old truck," I commented. "It would take me a week to shovel this driveway."

"It'll be nice to see the spring again, eh boys? Get out there on the river, catch a salmon or two," mused Stan. "Next year, I'm gonna spend more time on the river."

"I don't know how a lad could spend any more time than he does already, without sleeping on it," I said.

"I slept on 'er many nights," lied Stan. "Just lying back in the canoe, drifting along. One night I fell asleep in the canoe and ended up on the rocks down in the Gray Rapids. Eleven miles! Took me the rest of the night and half the day to pole back home."

"Is that the same day you caught the forty-pounder?" asked Lindon.

"No, I believe that was the day before."

"Got it on a little Butterfly," I put in.

"Got it on a little Butterfly," said Stan.

"Took ya all afternoon to land it," said Lindon.

"Took me all afternoon to land it," said Stan.

"Weighed more than forty pounds, didn't it, Stan?"

"Yes, yes, I think it did. Thinkin' back on it, I believe it weighed more like fifty."

It was about then that we heard another knock on my door. It was Nean Kooglin.

"Come in, Nean," I greeted him. "I hope you brought some rum."

"Rum? Rum? Would I show up on a night like this without rum?" said Nean, ducking his head so he could get through the door. "I was just glancing through the *Digest* and came upon this nice set of Striker golf clubs. I was thinking I need a new set and might send for them." Nean pulled out a page from his magazine and handed it to me. "The ones at the top of the page. What d'ya think?"

"Good looking clubs," I said. "You have lots of time to think about it."

"Yeah, well. It's a hell of a night, but I got to thinkin' about golf and couldn't make up my mind, so . . . thought maybe they'd do something for my game."

"Well, come in and sit down," I said. "Tonight is definitely the right time to discuss it."

"I was just telling Lindon and Lute about the big salmon I caught," announced Stan.

"The forty-pounder?"

"That's right, Nean. Only it was more like fifty."

"Got 'im on a Cosseboom, didn't ya?"

"Could've been a Cosseboom," said Stan. "I just forget. Either a Cosseboom or a Dusty Rat."

"Butterfly, I believe," said Lindon.

"That's right, that's right. It was a Butterfly. I remember it now. A little double."

"That reminds me," I said. "I invented a new fly awhile ago."

I picked my newly invented fly from the curtain where I'd left it and showed it to them.

"Good lookin' fly," said Nean.

"Thought it might work when there's a few clouds around," I said.

"It might at that," said Lindon. "A blue body. Never seen a fly quite like it. You, Stan?"

"Well, now, come to think of it, I have. Yes sir! I tied a few just like that a couple of years ago. Caught a lot of fish on it, too. As a matter of fact, I think that's the fly I caught nineteen salmon on in one afternoon," said Stan.

"Was it a cloudy day?" asked Lindon.

"Well, yes, I believe it was. Yes sir, I caught nineteen salmon in one afternoon and not one of them was a grilse, not one of them was small enough to keep. Caught them on a fly the very same as that little one right there."

"So what do you call it?" I asked.

"Let me see . . . I just don't recall. What did I call it? What did I call that little devil? Hmm."

"A Snowflake?" suggested Nean.

"Yes! By God, you got it. That's exactly what I called it! A Snowflake."

"What d'ya say we have a game of cards, boys?" I suggested.

Everyone was up for a card game, and that's what we did for most of the night.

As far as the fly goes, I really wasn't sure if the pattern was unique in the world, anyway. Stan may have invented it, I may have invented it, or it may have been invented by someone a hundred years ago. Who knows? I do know, however, that Stan Tuney never caught nineteen salmon in one afternoon on it or any other fly. Stan just likes to hear himself talk. That's how he gets on stormy days.

Me? I get cynical. In the winter, I can't help but speak about my surroundings with irony and sarcasm. But it's just the winter and only the winter that makes me that way. I know the reality of my situation. Take me away from the Maritimes for more than a week or two and I'd be as curious as hell about what's happening here. We have great people here. They're the kind of people who will visit you on a stormy night and talk about golf, or about dace swimming between the surface and the golden bottom of the river. Somehow, down deep inside, I think it's wrong to move away for the winter. It's hard on the economy. When you've saved enough, go down south and spend it, but never mind, if you get sick, c'mon back. We'll look after you.

Well, the next time you hear from me, hopefully I'll have a fish story or two to tell. If I don't have any true ones, I'm sure I'll have a whole library of the fictional kind stored up. That's if the winter gets any worse than it's been already.

It's noon. Today is the first of January, a hundred and four and a half days until opening day on the river.

Luther Corhern

Fiction by Herb Curtis

The Americans Are Coming
The Silent Partner
The Brennen Siding Trilogy